I0687620

Broken Ties

by

Gloria Davidson Marlow

This is a work of fiction. Names, characters, places, and incidents are either the product of the author's imagination or are used fictitiously, and any resemblance to actual persons living or dead, business establishments, events, or locales, is entirely coincidental.

Broken Ties

COPYRIGHT © 2014 by Gloria Davidson Marlow

All rights reserved. No part of this book may be used or reproduced in any manner whatsoever without written permission of the author or The Wild Rose Press, Inc. except in the case of brief quotations embodied in critical articles or reviews.
Contact Information: info@thewildrosepress.com

Cover Art by *Debbie Taylor*

The Wild Rose Press, Inc.
PO Box 708
Adams Basin, NY 14410-0708
Visit us at www.thewildrosepress.com

Publishing History
First Crimson Rose Edition, 2014
Print ISBN 978-1-62830-479-4
Digital ISBN 978-1-62830-480-0

Published in the United States of America

With a comforting murmur, he pulled her against him. His breath ruffled her hair, and she slipped her arms around his waist. She nestled against him, drinking in the warm masculine scent of him and finding comfort in the way his arms wrapped protectively around her.

"Ah, Sidra," he whispered against her hair, and she answered by lifting her face to his, breathing his name against his mouth as she stood on tiptoe to touch her lips to his.

"Levi."

His eyes blazed and his mouth claimed hers hungrily. Desire unfurled deep within her, and she returned his kisses with equal ferocity. Her hands slipped inside his shirt, running over the smooth skin of his back as his cupped her head, holding her still for his deepening kisses.

"My God, I want you," he groaned, his thumbs stroking her face. "But we can't do this now."

Embarrassment warmed her face and she stepped back, trying to regain her composure. She had worked for this man for four years, kept her attraction to him hidden, and maintained her professionalism and thus her pride. Had she always been a mere breath away from losing control and throwing herself at him like a fool? And how many times did she need him to refuse what she was offering, before she quit?

Praise for Gloria Davidson Marlow

"*Sweet Sacrifices* grabs you right from the beginning and doesn't let go. A surprisingly good mystery with some suspense and clean romance adding interest to the story."

~*Vicki, Sizzling Hot Book Reviews (5 Hearts)*
~*~

"Turning a tangled web of deceit and pain into a sweet love story is not an easy thing to do. But that's exactly what Gloria Davidson Marlow does…. Immediately drawn to her characters and driven by the constant mystery surrounding them, I couldn't put the book down."

~*Rebecca, The Romance Reviews (4 Stars)*
~*~

"*Sweet Sacrifices* ensnares the reader's emotions and imagination with heartbreaking scenes of Kendal's past when she is at the mercy of circumstances she cannot control. However, Ms. Marlow creates compelling, interwoven subplots that reveal Kendall's strength, courage, and capacity to love as the story, so full of sacrifices, becomes a story of amazing, euphoric love that is strong, patient, and, true. This story shows the flaws and foibles of human nature, bit it, most of all, shows love that overcomes all."

~*Camellia, Long and Short Romance Reviews*
(4 Books)

Chapter One

Outside her office window the high school chorus launched into "Carol of the Bells," and Sidra Martin tossed her pencil on her desk with an exasperated sigh. She gave up. There would be no working in peace tonight or any other night for the next four weeks. Christmas was in full swing and, from here on out, it would be carols and lights at every turn. Her yearly neurosis would kick in, and she would live in an inexplicable state of fear and anxiety until the final Christmas carol was sung and the last string of lights was back in storage.

With a glance at the clock, she grabbed her fleece-lined coat from the rack behind the door and rushed to the elevator. If she didn't hurry, she'd miss the bus again, as she had every night for the last month. Thanks to Levi Tanner and his increasing demands, she stayed later and later every night. Not that she minded, really. She supposed spending her evenings with a real flesh-and-blood man was always better than spending them with the make-believe hero in a romance novel, a dog named Coda, and the unnamed calico cat that lived next door but had recently made itself at home with her, as well.

"Sidra!" Levi yelled, just as she had buttoned the last button on her coat and placed one high-heeled foot inside the elevator.

She sighed heavily and stepped back, letting the elevator doors slide closed as she went back to his office.

She expected to find Levi hunched over one of the files that littered his desk. Instead, he stood with his back to her, leaning against the window that overlooked the town square. One raised hand was flattened against the cold glass pane, and his shoulder muscles bunched beneath the light blue cotton of his shirt and pulled at the waistband of his khakis. The other hand was wrapped around a double shot of whiskey on the rocks. His dark hair gleamed in the light cast by the hundreds of colored bulbs outside his window, and he spoke softly without turning around.

"You missed it. They just lit the tree."

Coming to stand beside him, she glimpsed the lights and oversized ornaments hanging from the town's large evergreen. Fear wormed its way through her, the same old questions hammering at its heels. What would he think if he knew the sight of Christmas lights filled her with dread and she had no idea why?

"Was there something you needed?" She made no effort to hide her annoyance, and although it had as much to do with her own strange paranoia as his demands, she didn't tell him that. Let him think she was angry he'd kept her late again, or, she thought as she shot a disapproving look at the glass in his hand, because he was ending one more day with a drink that would leave him even more surly and impatient than usual.

"No. Sorry. Just feeling a bit nostalgic, I guess."

She softened at the sadness in his voice, studying his handsome face in the artificial glow. He looked more weary and worried tonight than usual, his cheeks hollow above his five o'clock shadow and a deepening furrow between his dark brows. The hurt he hid beneath his tough exterior showed more every day.

"Well, I've probably missed the bus anyway," she told him with forced lightness, "and the next one isn't for an hour and a half. Is there anything else you'd like to get done before I try leaving again?"

He turned toward her, his dark, shadowed eyes raking over her, taking in everything from her dark blond bob to her tweed heels, before settling on the leather gloves she still clasped in her hands.

"I never think of you taking the bus. Do you walk alone to the station every night?"

She looked around pointedly. It was only the two of them, now that Teddy was gone. The women who had worked here when she started four years ago were long gone, unable to cope with the bickering between the brothers. They had slipped away one by one, until she alone was left to prefer the sniping over the silence that had enveloped the office the last few months.

"Yes, I suppose you do," he murmured in answer to his question. "And Teddy knew that, didn't he? That's why he walked you out every day. That's why he didn't want you to go alone that night, why he kept insisting you should stay until we closed the office. It's why he offered to drive you home."

"Levi," she said, placing a comforting hand on his arm. He'd beat himself up long enough over his decisions the night of the accident. It was time for him to forgive himself.

Taking a deep breath, he pushed a long-fingered hand through his unruly hair. "Go home, Sidra. If you hurry, maybe you can still catch your bus."

"But—" She didn't want to leave him alone, not tonight when it was obvious he was in such a brooding, melancholy mood.

"I said go!" he barked, and she turned on her heel and strode back to the elevator.

She practically ran across the town square, pulling her collar up against the chill night air, the sounds of Christmas that drifted her way, and the feel of Levi's eyes burning holes in her back. Leave it to him to make her miss the bus for no good reason at all. Had he really called her back so she could see the lighting of the Christmas tree, of all things? In all the years she'd known him, she had never given him any reason to think she would want to see the town tree being lit. Of course, she'd never given him any reason to think she wouldn't, either.

As far as he knew, she was a normal girl with the same enthusiasm for the holidays everyone else had. Normal people wanted to see Christmas decorations and listen to holiday songs. At the very least, they wanted to gather close to the people they cared about and share the most wonderful time of year with the ones they loved. She had been trying to act normal for as long as she could remember. She had tried to smile and act excited, tried to sing the songs and dance the dances they forced on her every year in school, but more often than not she ended up in tears, huddled in a corner somewhere while the other kids performed. It hadn't really mattered, since there was no one in the audience to notice her absence and no one behind the scenes who cared.

All these years later, she still had no friends or

relatives to gather close about her or notice that she participated in the holidays in only the most superficial ways. She had never told anyone about the nearly debilitating fear that came upon her each holiday season or the breathless panic that seized her each and every time she caught a glimpse of the massive evergreen in the town square. She just rushed past it each year, closing her mind to the fear it caused.

As she turned the corner past the town square, the lights and sounds faded away, and she glanced at her watch. If she hurried and was lucky, she could still catch the bus to Barrington Station. From there, a bus ran to her Reynolds Park neighborhood. That would shave an hour off her wait for a bus that took the direct route home, and she much preferred the warmth of the bus to the cold darkness of the bus stop.

She had never been an exceptionally lucky person, so she wasn't surprised to see the tail lights of the Barrington Station bus disappearing around the far corner when she reached the stop. With a heavy sigh, she adjusted her purse and glanced around her. The diner across the street gleamed with light and warmth, and the windows decorated with multicolored bulbs and garland were the perfect frame for the diners within. There was no way she was waiting there. Nothing underscored a person's loneliness like being alone in the midst of a dozen laughing families and flirting couples.

She shivered violently as a particularly vicious gust of wind whipped around her, cutting through the sheer stockings she wore beneath her knee-length black pencil skirt. Perhaps the diner wasn't such a bad idea.

"Are you waiting on the seven-thirty to Reynolds

Park?"

Her heart skipped a beat at the sound of the thickly accented male voice, and she turned quickly, her breath catching in her throat as she met the stranger's dark gaze.

"Yes," she forced out, hooking a finger toward the café, "but we've decided to wait inside."

"We?" he asked, one thin eyebrow tilting sardonically.

"My husband is already there." Even to her own ears, it sounded like a lie.

"He left you here? All alone? In the dark?"

"He's a bit put out with me. We missed the early bus, and he thinks it's my fault."

She laughed, a hollow, high-pitched sound she barely recognized. Her hand went to her chest, as if to still her frantic heartbeat. What in the world was wrong with her? He was not the first stranger who had ever asked her a question at the bus stop. So why was she finding it so difficult to keep from running away? She laughed again, much too nervously, and offered him an apologetic smile.

"I'd better hurry. The longer he waits, the angrier he'll get."

"Of course." His mouth turned up in a smile that didn't come close to reaching the cold dark pools of his eyes, and a shiver of apprehension rushed up her spine.

Clutching her purse tightly in her hands, she turned away, intent on hurrying toward the diner. She lifted her hand as if waving to someone on the other side of the window as she stepped away from him.

Without warning, his large body pressed against her back, a cloth covered her mouth and nose, and she spiraled into chloroform-induced darkness.

"Wave good-bye, Princess," he whispered as she fell against him.

****

Levi watched Sidra hurry across the square, her caramel-blond curls blowing about her face as she pulled the collar of her coat up to block out the cold. The belt hugged her waist, accentuating her soft curves and the gentle sway of her hips, and he could almost hear the no-nonsense clip of her shoes as she quickened her pace, fleeing the Christmas pageantry like the hounds of hell were on her heels. He lifted his glass to his own hyperbole. Sidra had far too much dignity to flee anything. She would walk as sedately as possible, spine straight, head held high as if she were scared of nothing.

That's how she'd entered his life four years ago, when she followed Teddy into his office as if she already had the position he hadn't even known they were trying to fill.

Dressed in a brown plaid skirt, turtleneck sweater, and boots, she sat in the waiting area as he and Teddy argued over hiring her, their voices loud enough for the whole office to hear through the door of his office. And while they argued and she did her very best not to look their way, he watched her through the glass wall that separated his office from the rest.

She sat, legs crossed demurely, no sign she heard them other than the pink that crept up her cheeks as they continued. She was dressed conservatively, with not an inch of unnecessary flesh showing, yet the longer he watched her, the more attracted he became to her. Though that made him that much more determined not to hire her, in the end Teddy wore him down, and he gave in if for no other reason than to silence his younger brother's whining.

In the four years since that day, his attraction to her had never waned. She was efficient, classy and poised, but above everything else, Sidra Martin was a beautiful woman.

He took a long slow sip of whiskey, hoping the slow burn of it would dampen his desire and dilute the painful memories and loneliness that haunted him tonight.

He knew he'd been too harsh with Sidra, but he couldn't bear the sympathy in her deep brown eyes, the soft touch of her hand on his arm. He didn't deserve her kindness or her pity. No matter how badly she might want to, she couldn't fix him. She could never bridge the gap and ask his brother to forgive what was unforgivable.

Now, a movement behind her caught his eye and he pressed his face closer to the cold glass of the window. Something about the way the man slipped from the shadows as Sidra passed him made the hairs on the back of Levi's neck stand on end. When she disappeared around the far corner, and the man darted a look around him before slinking down the street behind her, Levi knew he had to follow them.

He reached for the drawer where he kept his gun, pausing only a moment before jerking it open and cupping the familiar weight of his pistol in his palm. Jamming it into his waistband, he rushed from the building and through the town square. He might be overly cautious, but better that than sorry. He had learned that lesson the hard way, and the experience had cost him and Teddy dearly. He wouldn't risk Sidra by playing it too safe this time around.

The street past the town square was empty when he turned the corner, and he picked up his pace. He was running by the time he took the left at the next block, and the bus station came into view. Sidra's back was to him as she spoke to the stranger, and Levi could almost feel her unease when the man stepped toward her. He wanted to yell out a warning as she turned away from the man, lifting her hand toward the diner as if she were waving at someone there, but before he could make a sound, the man closed the space between them. His arm snaked around her shoulder, his hand covering her face with a rag as her body crumpled against him.

"Sidra!" Levi yelled, drawing his gun and running toward them.

Without sparing him a glance, her assailant hoisted Sidra over his shoulder and ran toward the back of the platform.

Frightened he'd hit her if he shot at the man, Levi continued his pursuit, firing into the air as he closed in on them. The man stumbled, the weight of his burden throwing him off balance so that he landed on his knees on the platform.

Mere yards away, Levi commanded him to put her down, while the man struggled to stand with Sidra still over his shoulder. Finally, with a vicious curse, he let her slip to the ground and darted away.

Levi reached the edge of the platform just as a dark sedan peeled from the alleyway behind the station and sped down the street.

A soft curse escaped him as he turned back to Sidra. He knelt beside her, feeling for a pulse and breathing a sigh of relief when his fingers felt the steady beating at the base of her neck. A glimmer of gold near her hair caught his attention, and he picked the coin up, to study the design with sickening recognition.

"Is she all right?" a woman called to him, and he looked up.

A group of people hurried toward them from the diner.

"We thought we heard shots," one of the men said. "The police are on their way."

As if on cue, a siren sounded in the distance.

"She's just fainted. She'll be fine," Levi answered before slipping the coin into his pocket, scooping Sidra up in his arms and hurrying away.

Chapter Two

Sidra's eyes fluttered open, and she sat up with a cry of alarm.

"Steady, Sweetheart."

Relief at hearing Levi's low, soothing voice instead of the accented voice of the stranger made her weak with relief, and tears sprang to her eyes. Without warning, she threw her arms around him.

"I've got you," he murmured, his arms coming around her, holding her shaking body against him as she savored the warmth and strength of his embrace.

Levi could be demanding, exasperating and abrasive, but he was also handsome, caring and gentle. She had been half in love with him since the day Teddy brought her to the office, introduced her to Levi, and announced he was hiring her. Levi had protested mightily, but Teddy stood firm. In the end, she thought, even Levi was glad he had. After all, she was all that remained in the aftermath of their final blow-up and those dreadful moments when everything had changed.

She pulled away from him, sitting back against the brown suede sofa as her eyes roamed the room around her. They were in the loft apartment where he lived above the Tanner & Tanner Investigations office, a space she had been in only a handful of times, and never when he was here. She'd been sent up to get coffee when they ran out downstairs, retrieve a sandwich or some other item he'd forgotten to bring down, or use the telephone while they waited for a repairman to fix the one in the office.

"I need you to tell me exactly what happened tonight." Although Levi spoke in the quiet, coaxing tone he used with the most nervous of witnesses, she knew it was more command than request.

The pale glow of the Christmas lights once again reflected in his dark eyes, and a sudden chill shook her. She pulled her knees up to her chest, wrapping her arms around them protectively.

"A man came up to me. I tried to tell him someone was waiting in the diner for me, but he grabbed me and put a rag over my face. I don't know what happened then. I don't know what he did after that." An edge of hysteria crept into her voice, and she took a shuddering breath, trying to calm her racing heart.

"Nothing else happened," he said, his dark gaze softening when she looked at him. "I saw him follow you around the corner. I was worried, so I went after you. I was almost to you when I saw him grab you. He picked you up and tried to run, but he dropped you. You'll probably be sore as hell tomorrow. But that's it. He didn't have time to do anything else."

She couldn't speak past the lump in her throat, so she nodded her head in understanding. Thank God Levi had decided to follow her. She hated to think what could have happened if he hadn't.

"The two of you were talking when I came around the corner. What were you saying?"

"He asked if I was waiting for the bus to Reynolds Park, and I told him yes."

"Reynolds Park? How did he know that's where

you were going?"

"I figured it was a lucky guess. I'd just missed the bus to Barrington Station, so the next logical guess would be Reynolds Park."

"That makes sense." He paused. "Have you ever seen him before?"

"No."

"Did he say anything to make you think you were more than just a random victim?"

"You mean, some proof he wouldn't have taken just any girl who happened to be there?"

"Yes."

"No, I don't think so. Why? Do you think he wanted me specifically?"

"I'm not sure, but I'm leaning that way."

"What? Why?"

"Because there was a car waiting for him, and he wasn't the driver. They pulled away too fast for him to have been the driver. It had to have been waiting out of sight for him to bring you there."

"Why in the world would someone target me, of all people?" That was the craziest idea she had ever heard, but she could tell he believed it, at least partly.

"I don't know. Do you?"

She shook her head. "No. But I'm not even sure I believe that's the case. I think he was probably just some sicko looking for a victim."

"No, something's off in that scenario. He didn't look like someone looking for a victim."

"What did he look like, then?"

"He looked like an assassin looking for a target."

She laughed nervously. "You've been watching too many action movies."

"I'm telling you, there was something too calculated and well-rehearsed about it all for me to think it was a chance abduction."

"Because he had a car waiting for him? Maybe he's just some rich guy with a driver who helps him get his kicks."

"How often are you alone there at the bus stop this time of night?"

"I'm usually there earlier, but I've been late every night this week. I've taken the bus to Barrington Station instead of Reynolds Park, where I live."

"If he's been watching you, he would know that."

She shivered with fear. Had someone been watching her?

"Have you noticed anything out of the ordinary at home or anywhere else?"

"No." She gasped as something came to mind. "Yes. Just last week, a car was parked outside my house for a while. It was a dark four-door sedan with tinted windows. I thought it was someone doing surveillance on my neighbor. He's in the middle of a lawsuit, and his attorney warned him it might happen. He knows where I work and that you do that sort of thing, so he asked me about it. I confirmed it, and two days later the car was there in the road. Do you think that could it have been the same man?"

"Anything's possible, and we aren't taking any chances. If this guy has been stalking you, he knows where you live and work. He probably even knows where you spend your spare time."

"Stalking me?" she squeaked.

"Yes. I'd say he's probably been doing it for a while and knew you would be at the bus station tonight.

If not in time for the early bus, then the late one. He didn't just guess where you were going. He already knew."

She felt the blood drain from her face. Was that why he'd seemed so familiar? Why his voice alone sent shivers of fear through her?

"He'll never get that close to you again, Sid. I promise you that."

"I told him my husband was in the diner, that I was meeting him there. No wonder he laughed. If he's been following me, he knows I don't have a husband or anyone else waiting for me. He must know I'm all alone."

"You aren't all alone." His voice was gruff as he moved to kneel in front of her. He cupped her face in his hands and placed a soft kiss on her forehead. "I'm right here with you, and I'm not letting anyone hurt you."

"He knew me," she whispered. "And I think I knew him."

"What do you mean? You know who he is?"

She shook her head. "No, not him. But something about him. It was familiar."

A chill swept through her, and she closed her eyes against the terror it brought.

"Tell me what you think you know about him."

"He had a very thick accent."

"What kind of accent? Spanish? French?"

She shook her head as he ran through a list of the most common languages. "No. Closer to French, maybe, but I'm not sure."

"Did he say anything in another language? Maybe we could have a translator tell us what language it was."

"Good-bye, Princess. *Adieu, princesse.*" The foreign words formed on the tip of her tongue, and she closed her eyes tightly as they spilled from her of their own accord. When she opened her eyes, her heart was pounding and she was shaking like a leaf. She had not only just spoken a language she'd never heard before tonight, she'd understood it when the stranger spoke it. How had she only just realized that he hadn't spoken English at all?

"I have to go home." Panic made her speak in short, quick breaths as she surged to her feet, and her eyes searched the room for her coat and purse. "Where are my things?"

"You aren't going home." His tone brooked no argument, but she ignored that fact as she caught sight of her belongings.

Her hands shook so badly she could barely grasp the strap of her purse, but she somehow managed to loop it over her shoulder and head for the door.

"Good-bye, Levi. Thank you for your help."

At his bark of laughter, she looked back to find him shoving his arms into the sleeves of his coat, dark eyes burning with fury.

"I hope you don't really think I'd let you leave here alone. If you're going home, I'm going with you."

"What do you mean?"

"I mean just what I said. You aren't leaving here alone. I'm staying the night with you, tonight and every night, until I'm certain no one is after you."

Although she knew she should protest, she remained silent as her knees went weak with relief. Thankfully, he placed a hand at her elbow and led her back to the sofa before she could crumple into a helpless, quivering heap.

"Stay here," he commanded. "I have to pack a bag."

She closed her eyes as he left the room, and the stranger's voice whispered through her mind.

Good-bye, Princess.

She felt the large hand close over her mouth as his arm came around her waist, lifting her off her feet. The doll she'd been holding slipped from her grasp and fell to the floor, the sparkle of Christmas lights dancing across its vinyl skin and blond hair.

"Mama!" she tried to scream, but the sound was muffled as he dashed through the door to the car waiting just beyond the drive.

"Wave good-bye, Princess," he said as he yanked open the back door and shoved her inside the vehicle.

Chapter Three

"No!" Sidra cried, springing upright.

Levi rushed into the room, gun drawn. He breathed a sigh of relief when he realized she was safe, but worry filled him as he took in her pallor and the dazed look in her eyes.

"What is it?" he demanded as he holstered the gun.

"It's happened before." Shock made her voice low, emotionless, and she stared into the distance.

"What do you mean, it's happened before? Why the hell didn't you tell me?" Anger surged through him, making his voice gruffer than he intended. His fingers closed over her arms. "I would never have let you walk out alone. I would have protected you, Sidra. Didn't you know that?"

She shook her head slowly, confusion darkening her eyes, and he cursed long and loud as he leapt to his feet and began to pace the room. Why hadn't she told him before now? How could she not have known he would do all he could to keep her safe?

"No, Levi. No." She shook her head again, some color returning to her face. "I think I was a child the first time."

He stopped mid-stride and stared at her. "You think? What does that mean?"

"It means I'm not sure it actually happened or if I just imagined it."

"So this is something you just remembered or imagined tonight?"

She nodded, her teeth catching at her bottom lip.

He let out a long breath, trying to focus on this new idea.

"Okay. Well, let's assume it's true. How old were you?"

"Young. Maybe five or six years old. I don't know."

"How old are you now?"

"Twenty-six?"

He didn't miss the questioning tone in her voice.

"Are you telling me or asking me?"

"Neither," she said with a heavy sigh. "I can't tell you because I don't know. I wouldn't ask you because you don't know."

"What do you mean, you don't know?"

"I was discovered alone in the restroom of a rest area on I-95 near Orlando. The woman who found me there took me to the local authorities, but no one ever claimed me, and I spent the rest of my childhood in foster care."

"What about before then?"

"I don't remember anything before that."

"Nothing at all?"

"I remember bits and pieces, things I'm not sure are memories. They might be just wishful thinking." She smiled ruefully and shook her head. "I've always had one particular memory of a pretty brown-haired woman with a wide smile and kind blue eyes. My heart wants to believe she's my mother, but I've never understood how someone who looks so kind and loving could leave her child alone on the side of the road. I have a vague recollection of a bedroom with tiny purple flowers on the wallpaper and a white canopy bed with a ruffled spread. And I think I remember riding a carousel on a brilliant green lawn. I've always had a penchant for fairy tales, daydreaming about being someone else, so no one's ever given much credence to my recollections. Not even me."

At the wistfulness in her voice, Levi had to fight the urge to pull her into his arms. It broke his heart to imagine a little girl with blond hair and large brown eyes, alone and frightened, tossed aside by parents who didn't want her.

He and Teddy had grown up in Gulfview, a small town near the Gulf of Mexico, in a drafty Victorian they shared with their parents, younger sister, and spinster aunt. Their paternal grandparents lived in a small farmhouse outside the city limits, and at least a dozen other Tanners were spread through town. He couldn't imagine growing up with no family at all. Just the past few months of self-imposed exile had nearly killed him.

"I lived in homes all over the state. Some of them were filled with other kids, but in most of them, it was either only me or just one other child. The others always stayed behind when I left, and I never saw them again."

She was staring at her hands, which were clutched so tightly the knuckles were white, and he felt a sick dread in the pit of his stomach as he wondered just what kind of life she had lived in the homes of strangers. Had she had any stability in her life? Had she ever had anyone who loved her?

"Did you change homes much?" he asked, hoping

he was wrong in his suspicions of how alone she had really been.

"I was fifteen when I ran away from one home. It was number thirteen." She tried to smile, but failed miserably. "Turns out it was as unlucky as you'd expect."

He couldn't bring himself to ask her to elaborate, so he focused on the number of homes she'd been in instead.

"Thirteen homes? That couldn't have given you time to form any kind of bonds with anyone in any of them. Did you ever have anyone constant?"

"Only Carlotta, the woman who took me to and from each new home, and she would check up on me every few months. She would decide if I stayed or left, and more often than not, I left." She took a shuddering breath before continuing. "She retired the year before I aged out of foster care, but she called me a few times the first few years, just to see how I was doing. She's in a nursing home now."

"Did she ever suspect you may have been kidnapped as a child?"

"She never mentioned it, and until now I never considered it."

"Tell me what makes you think it happened."

Levi watched her intently as she described what she thought was a memory. Her brandy-colored eyes grew dark with fear and confusion, and he wished he could ease her mind, but he had no idea what to say. No empty platitude or lame assurance was going to make her feel better or heal the pain of the past.

She had worked for him for four years. How could he not have known something so important about her?

Part of the reason he was good at his job was his ability to read people, to gauge their sincerity and state of mind. Yet he had never once noticed the hint of sadness that tinged her eyes or the way she hid behind that quiet, reserved grace of hers, using it like a shield to keep him from seeing any flicker of need. He had lost all objectivity the first time she spoke his name in that soft, lilting voice of hers and placed her delicate hand in his. His immediate flicker of attraction had burst into flames, and he had been blinded by his desire and his certain knowledge that she belonged to Teddy.

That had been the first bone of contention between him and his brother, and from there, it had all gone downhill. By the time everything went to hell in a handbasket, Sidra was the only one left, he was half in love with her, and he couldn't imagine how he would have dealt with all of it without her.

Just like the day he met her and hundreds of days since, all he could think of now was how much he wanted to kiss those soft, full lips.

"Are you even listening to me?" she asked, cocking her head to one side.

Without considering the consequences, he lowered his mouth to hers and kissed her with years of pent-up passion.

****

She had been kissed a time or two in the past, but never so deeply and thoroughly as this. And never had she welcomed a kiss so much. He knew it, too, judging by the low growl that sounded in his throat as he deepened the kiss.

When at last they broke apart, they were both breathless and dazed by the desire that arced between them. Even as she was trying to gather her composure, she felt him pull away from her, saw his eyes darken with remorse.

"Sid, I'm sorry," he said. "I shouldn't have done that. You're scared and vulnerable, and I took advantage of it."

"You're sorry you kissed me?" She wished she didn't sound quite so horrified by his words.

"Yes. No. Jeeze, Sid. I'm sorry I kissed you *now*. You were nearly kidnapped tonight. You were knocked out by chloroform. You couldn't possibly be in your right mind."

"So you think I kissed you back because my judgment was compromised by my being chloroformed?" She fought to regain a grip on her dignity.

"Yes."

"I've thought about kissing you an awful lot before today." That admission was proof of just how far gone her mind was at the moment.

"You have?" He sounded like a vulnerable schoolboy, shocked that the object of his crush reciprocated his feelings.

A smile spread across her face, and she nodded.

"Yes. And I've never been chloroformed before."

"But Teddy—"

Frustration bubbled up inside her as the smile slipped from her face. How long was he going to cling to his foolish notion that she and Teddy were more than friends? They had never given him any reason to believe it. Yet, he had never been able to get past his own stupid assumptions that they were lovers. She opened her mouth to tell him just what she thought about his pigheaded refusal to see the truth, but before she could speak, he stood and moved to the kitchen.

He came back moments later with a glass of whiskey in one hand and a can of soda in the other. He set the soda on the end table nearest her and swallowed the whiskey in one gulp.

"None of it matters now," he said, slamming the glass down on the table and raking a hand through his hair. "We can't afford a distraction like this."

"Will we be any less attracted to each other if we ignore it?" She frowned at the empty glass. "Or if you're drunk?"

"I don't know. What I do know is that I need to keep all my attention on protecting you from the man who tried to take you. From here on out, we have to control whatever it is we feel for each other. We have to move forward with clear minds. And I'm not drunk."

"Levi," she protested, but was silenced when he kissed her again, before pulling her to her feet, taking her bag and leading her downstairs, gun at the ready.

Feeling as if her head were stuffed with fuzz, she leaned back against the headrest in his car and closed her eyes.

"Are you okay?" he asked as he climbed behind the wheel.

"Not really." She rolled her head to look at him.

He reached for her hand where it lay on the seat between them.

"We'll find whoever's behind this, Sid. Don't worry."

She wondered if he realized he still said "we" as if he and Teddy continued to work together and nothing had ever come between them. She didn't mention that as she offered him a half-hearted smile.

"I know," she assured him. She knew he would try, even if she wasn't sure he'd be successful.

Except for her directions, they were silent on the way to her house, and she was grateful for the time to think. She had wondered a million times over the years what had driven her parents to leave her at that rest area. Now, for the first time, she wondered if there had been a reason she was there other than them not wanting her. Had they been foreigners? Was that how she knew a language she didn't remember ever hearing? Had they escaped to America? Had they been illegal? Forced to run from the immigration authorities and leave her behind? Had they been arrested, or deported back to their homeland? Or had she really been kidnapped?

He slowed as they turned onto her road, and she pointed at the two-bedroom postwar home she'd rented three years ago. She frowned at the light in the living room window. She didn't remember leaving it on, but she'd been in a hurry this morning, running late because she couldn't find one of her shoes. She must have rushed out as soon as she found it behind the sofa, not even remembering to turn out the light as she scolded Coda on her way out the door.

"Nice place," Levi said as they walked up the shrub-lined pathway to the carport. "But these shrubs need to come up. Someone could easily hide behind them."

"Thanks. I like it. And I like the shrubs. They're staying right where they are. I'd have to get the landlord's approval before I pulled them up anyway."

Coda's whining turned to furious barking as Sidra

turned the key in the lock and pushed open the door. What in the world was wrong with the crazy dog? Did she know Levi was here? Did she think Teddy was nearby, too?

Sidra had barely pushed the door open when Coda flew through it, barking up a storm as she launched herself at Levi's legs. Even in the dim glow of the porch light, Sidra saw Levi's face pale as he dropped to his knees to pet his brother's brown-and-white English bulldog.

"He left her with you?" he murmured.

"Mm-hmm."

She didn't trust herself to speak as she turned away from Levi's anguished eyes. It was beyond her understanding how two men who loved each other so much could cause each other so much pain.

She stopped before she entered her house, a gasp escaping her as she saw the mess illuminated by the dim light in the corner.

Chapter Four

Levi was on his feet in an instant, pushing Sidra behind him as he drew his gun and stepped inside. His eyes scanned the room, taking in the upended furniture, stopping at the curio cabinet lying on its side in the corner. Bits of brightly colored fabric stuck up from the broken glass and the paperbacks knocked from the nearby bookshelf.

As he moved from the living room to the kitchen and bedrooms, Sidra followed on his heels, fingers hooked through his belt loop, keeping him from getting too far ahead of her.

The kitchen cabinets hung open and the contents of the drawers had been emptied on the floor. The bedrooms weren't nearly as bad as the living room, or even the kitchen. Although the drawers had been emptied and their contents scattered about the floor, at least the beds were still made and the furniture was still in its upright position.

The second of the two bedrooms was obviously Sidra's. The dressing table was covered with cosmetics and perfume bottles, and the bed rumpled as if she'd sat on the side after making it up. His eyes fell on the bedside table, where a romance novel lay open beside the crystal carafe of water and the old-fashioned alarm clock beside it. As she lay in her bed all alone, did she imagine she was the heroine in a novel? Did she long for a man to sweep her off her feet, deposit her on the flowered quilt, and make love to her all night? Would she throw her head back like the cover model's, letting his mouth close over the throbbing pulse of her throat, or the delicate white skin above the plunging neckline of her soft blue gown? Did his quiet, efficient little secretary lose her sense of propriety when a man touched her like that? Would she have that look of pleasure on her face if it was his dark head bent over her, his breath warming her flesh?

He was so caught up in his own fantasies he hardly noticed she had turned loose of him and had become a whirling dervish, stuffing clothing back into drawers before slamming them into place with angry thumps.

Tears tracked her cheeks and her breath came in short, angry sobs as she worked. She was quickly coming undone, and he wasn't quite sure how to stop it without touching her. At the moment, however, touching her was not the best idea. He wanted to move toward her, take her in his arms, and soothe her, but he wasn't sure he could keep from giving in to his wayward imaginings. One day soon, he just might sweep her up and carry her to bed, but it wouldn't be tonight.

When she shoved the last drawer into place, she swung around to face him.

"Why would someone do this?" she demanded. "I have nothing to hide. Nothing anyone in the world besides me would want."

He had no idea how to answer her. The sliver of hope that the man really had picked her randomly because she had been at the bus stop died the moment they entered her house. There was no longer any doubt

Sidra was a target. The question was whose, and what did they intend to do to her once they had her. Dread became a rock-hard knot in his stomach as she continued to stare at him, questions burning in her eyes.

"I don't know, Sid, but I promise you we'll find whoever did this."

"You keep saying that, Levi, but I'm pretty sure he'll find us before we find him," she retorted as she pushed past him. "After all, he knows who he's looking for and exactly where to find me."

He followed her to the living room, where she began trying to straighten the mess the intruder had created.

"Help," she ordered, motioning to the upended bookshelf, which he lifted with ease.

She began plucking items from the broken glass of the curio cabinet while he set the sofa, easy chair, and tables upright. He turned back to find her setting a half dozen porcelain dolls, each dressed in a flowing jewel-toned gown, on the shelf, at perfect angles to the romance novels she'd already placed in neat, symmetrical rows. He shook his head in surprise. He would never have imagined Sidra as the fairytale-believing, doll-collecting type, but he couldn't deny the proof before his eyes. Romance novels and princess dolls were a dead giveaway of a hopeless romantic.

As she set the last doll on the shelf, she lost her grip on it, bobbling the figurine a moment before catching it. The tiny gold crown fell off the doll's head and landed on the floor at her feet. With a sigh, she bent to scoop it up, but stopped suddenly, seeming to stumble before sinking to her knees.

"Sid?" He rushed toward her as she braced her free

hand against the floor and squeezed her eyes closed tightly.

"Wave good-bye, Princess." The man shoved her into the back seat of the car and Sidra fell across a woman's lap. The tiara slipped from her head and landed with a soft thud beside the sensible pumps the woman wore. The woman bent to retrieve it as Sidra scrambled up the back seat, tears streaming down her cheeks while she watched her home grow smaller and smaller in the rear window.

"Mama! Papa!" she cried, her small fists pounding on the glass.

As they rounded the corner that hid the castle completely from view, the woman spoke with the same guttural accent as the man.

"Sit down, Princess. You will never see your parents again."

"Sidra?" Levi was kneeling beside her, his hand gentle on her back. "Are you okay?"

She nodded and pushed herself to her feet. "I'm fine."

He came to his feet, his eyes searching her face as he put an arm around her and led her to the sofa. She was shaking, her heart was beating frantically, and she could feel the tears on her cheeks.

"What happened?" he asked.

"A memory, a flashback. I don't know. Maybe just a vivid daydream."

"And?"

"And...I think I'm a princess."

"A what?"

"A princess. You know, a girl whose father is king and mother is queen?"

"I know what a princess is, Sid. I just don't know what makes you think you could be one."

"I was wearing a crown when I was kidnapped. I remember it fell off and landed by a lady's feet."

"Don't a lot of little girls wear crowns when they're playing? My niece loves to pretend she's a princess."

"Yes, but this one wasn't plastic and rhinestones."

"How can you know that?"

"I just do," she insisted. "I saw my home, Levi, and it was a castle."

"A castle?"

"I am not explaining to you what a castle is."

He chuckled and touched her hair while she waited with bated breath to see if he believed her.

"I can picture you in a crown and a castle," he admitted. "I just can't imagine how a princess came to be alone beside an American interstate. We don't have royalty here."

"I know that, Levi. But the woman in the car spoke the same language as the man who accosted me. Obviously I wasn't born here in America."

"So there was a woman involved?"

Had he even heard what she said?

"Yes, she was waiting in the car for us."

"What did she say?"

"She called me 'Princess' and told me I would never see my mother and father again." She bit her lip to fight back the tears that threatened. "I guess she was right."

With a comforting murmur, he pulled her against him. His breath ruffled her hair, and she slipped her arms around his waist. She nestled against him, drinking in the warm masculine scent of him and finding comfort in the way his arms wrapped protectively around her.

"Ah, Sidra," he whispered against her hair, and she answered by lifting her face to his, breathing his name against his mouth as she stood on tiptoe to touch her lips to his.

"Levi."

His eyes blazed and his mouth claimed hers hungrily. Desire unfurled deep within her, and she returned his kisses with equal ferocity. Her hands slipped inside his shirt, running over the smooth skin of his back as his cupped her head, holding her still for his deepening kisses.

"My God, I want you," he groaned, his thumbs stroking her face. "But we can't do this now."

Embarrassment warmed her face and she stepped back, trying to regain her composure. She had worked for this man for four years, kept her attraction to him hidden, and maintained her professionalism and thus her pride. Had she always been a mere breath away from losing control and throwing herself at him like a fool? And how many times did she need him to refuse what she was offering, before she quit?

"You must be starving," she announced, proud of the steadiness of her voice. "I'll fix us something to eat."

"Sid," he said, reaching for her arm.

She sidestepped him and went to the kitchen, relieved when he didn't follow.

She heard him move to the sofa, followed by the soft murmur of the television. With a shaky sigh, she sank into a chair and leaned her head on the table. The events of the night played through her head for the hundredth time, from the moment she'd left the office until now.

The man, the woman, the castle; it was all familiar, yet unknown. She had no idea what it meant. Was there any possible way she could be a princess? Or was she just a little girl playing dress-up like Levi suspected? Did she know the language they spoke firsthand, or was it only through her parents speaking it in the years before they abandoned her? Had she been abandoned, or had she been kidnapped? No one kidnapped a child only to leave them alone at a roadside service station. Did they?

Finally, when she accepted that she was missing too many pieces of the puzzle to solve it tonight, she stood up and moved to the stove. She started two grilled cheese sandwiches, then took out a plastic container of leftover vegetable soup and popped it into the microwave over the stove. She only cooked a few nights a week, ate leftovers a day or two, and sometimes froze a serving or two for later. The soup had been made yesterday and would probably be even better tonight than it had been then.

Peas porridge hot, peas porridge cold. The old nursery rhyme, recited in a thickly accented female voice, danced through her head. She tried to grasp hold of a solid memory to go with it, anything at all that would tell her who had spoken it. She came up with nothing at all.

Forcing herself away from the problem, she ladled soup into two ceramic bowls, which she placed on matching plates along with a handful of saltines and a sandwich each.

Levi entered the room as she set the plates on the table, and they ate in near silence. She couldn't understand why the attraction they'd felt for the last four years had suddenly become such a palpable presence between them, threatening to swallow them whole with the least provocation.

"The guest room bed is made up for you." She carried her dishes to the sink, praying he'd just go to bed without a fuss. She was too tired to try to hash out whether they'd crossed the line between employer and employee, acquaintances to lovers or whatever they had been to each other to what they were now.

"I'll sleep on the couch, Sid." When she would have protested, he explained. "I need to be near the door."

"I'll get you a blanket and pillow, then."

She hurried to the linen closet in the hallway. For a long moment, she stared blindly at the blankets and sheets folded neatly on the shelves. *Who I am?* That question had haunted her for so many years before she finally pushed it away, silencing it by creating a woman who knew who she was, or could at least pretend to know. She pressed trembling fingers to her temple. How could she be less certain of her identity now than she had been before?

"Why don't you do what you need to do to get ready for bed? I can make up the couch."

She nodded in agreement, then trudged to the bathroom to bathe before covering her modest flannel gown with a robe. She had never had a man sleep at her house, and it made her more nervous to have him here than she would have thought.

She entered the living room to find him sound

asleep, his head leaned back against the arm of the sofa and his eyes closed. A smile turned up the corners of her mouth, and she bent to pull his soft leather deck shoes from his feet. She carefully lifted his legs onto the cushions and settled a soft fleece throw over him. Before moving away, she brushed a dark lock of hair from his forehead and pressed her lips where it had been.

"Good night," she whispered.

"Night," he murmured, settling deeper into the sofa without opening his eyes.

It was surreal to have him here, kissing her one minute and pushing her away the next, sleeping on her sofa with Coda and the calico kitten curled up at his feet and his gun on the coffee table, so near he could snatch it up in seconds if need be.

She turned away, unwilling to think of why he might need the gun or imagine the moment he might use it to protect her or himself. He wouldn't hesitate this time. She knew him well enough to know that. That moment when he had hesitated, when he waited to fire a shot, was what had cost him his brother, and he would be determined not to let that happen again. She prayed they never found themselves in that situation.

"Go to bed, Sidra." The sound of his voice made her jump, and she glared at him. His eyes were mere slits, but his voice was deep and reassuring as he promised, "I've got this."

"Thank you," she said quietly, before turning toward her bedroom. Once in bed, she did her best not to imagine a stranger there, rummaging through things, looking for God alone knew what. She worked equally hard to keep from imagining Levi joining her in bed, his shirt unbuttoned and his eyes dark with passion.

****

Levi put an arm over his eyes, trying not to remember the taste of her lips or the way she felt in his arms. Most of the women he'd dated over the years wanted nothing more than he did, a few months of monogamy, sex while they saw each other, and a fond farewell that might or might not be permanent when the fun was over. None of them had wanted anything serious, and he had been more than willing to comply with their wishes. Sidra, however, was different. Whatever happened between them would change his life forever.

He peeked under his arm at the bookshelf where the princess dolls stared down at him with serene, knowing smiles. If the romance novels weren't enough to convince him, the benevolent smiles on their porcelain faces told him all he needed to know. He was beginning to suspect that, despite her own sad past, Sidra believed in fairytales and happy endings. He didn't know the first thing about fairytales, and he had no idea how to even begin giving her a happy ending.

Chapter Five

"Sidra!"

Her heart stopped and she stumbled from the shower to the bathroom door, wrapping a towel around her body as she went.

"What is it?" she cried as she rushed down the hall to the living room, where he stood with his back to her.

"Where's your computer?"

He turned toward her, his face registering complete shock when he saw her dripping wet and naked except for the towel. His eyes blazed with passion and he swallowed hard several times, as if trying to find his voice.

"What the hell are you doing?" he finally croaked.

"I was in the shower!" she retorted. "I thought something was wrong when I heard you yelling."

"Oh." His voice was tight and pained, and she felt a small surge of power. "Sorry."

"Was there something you needed?"

"Yeah, where's your computer?" he repeated, looking around the room. She wondered if he was still looking for a computer or just trying to avoid looking at her.

"I don't have one."

You don't have a computer?" he asked incredulously, his gaze landing on her before darting away again.

37

"Nope." She took another step toward him, letting her voice turn soft and sultry. "I have better things to do with my spare time than social networking and surfing the Internet."

"Like what?" He took another step back, and she allowed a smile to slip across her face.

"Reading, walking, volunteering at the nursing home. In my opinion, making houses out of toothpicks is a better way to spend time than staring at the computer."

"Really?" His gaze still moved about, trying to find something, anything, to land on but her.

"Mm-hmmm." She was close enough to press herself against him, but she held back as his labored breathing filled the small space that separated them. He was disturbed by her proximity and, most likely, by her totally uncharacteristic forwardness. Good. It served him right for scaring her half to death with all that yelling.

"Sidra," he groaned, "go put some clothes on. Now. Please."

She chuckled triumphantly and stepped back.

His hand shot out like lightning to snag the towel and pull her toward him. The edges of the towel came apart, so that her damp, naked body was pressed to him.

"Think you're funny, do you?" he growled against her mouth as he caught it in a kiss.

She smiled against his lips, and he let the towel drop to the floor behind her. Her protests were weak, at best, as his hands ran over her bare backside, cupping it and lifting her higher against him. She wrapped her legs around his waist as he carried her toward her bedroom.

He laid her back on the bed, trailing kisses from

her mouth to the bottom of her throat. His tongue teased the soft pulse throbbing there, and his hands moved in soft waves over her waist and hips.

Her hands fumbled at the button of his jeans, and he sat back, catching them in his own.

"Sidra, I—"

"Don't say it," she commanded, pulling her hands from his. "I haven't been chloroformed today, I'm not hysterical, and I am a woman completely capable of making this decision on my own."

"We need—"

"To concentrate. I know." The button popped open, and she smiled. "But I don't think either one of us can concentrate on anything until we get this out of the way."

His eyes slid closed at her touch, and he sighed. When they opened, the black depths were dark with desire and she knew there was no turning back, even if she wanted to. Their mouths met again as he pressed her back against the bed, his body claiming hers as she had dreamed of nearly every night for the last four years.

****

Dazed and satiated, Levi lay in Sidra's bed, listening to the shower running and the soft murmur of her singing. One arm rested over his eyes as he tried unsuccessfully to regret what had just happened. No matter how much he tried to scold himself, however, he couldn't muster up regret or apologies, and he doubted Sidra wanted either. She had obviously wanted it as badly as he had, if for no other reason than to get their attraction out of the way. He was smart enough to know that plan had backfired on them both. There was no way he could pretend his attraction to her had lessened. As a matter of fact, he was almost certain making love to her had only intensified it.

She had been every bit as receptive as he'd imagined she would be. He picked up the romance novel from the bedside table, studying the woman on the cover. Yes, Sidra had looked just as ecstatic and breathless as that woman, when his lips touched her neck. He could still taste the sweetness of her skin and feel the soft pulsing of her vein beneath his tongue, and the cover model's bosom didn't hold a candle to Sidra's.

"Are you reading that?" Her teasing voice interrupted his thoughts, and he tossed the book back onto the table, surprised to feel his face warm with embarrassment.

She stood in the doorway of the bathroom, fully dressed in jeans and a silky black shirt.

"You can have the shower now," she said, hooking a thumb over her shoulder.

"Are you going somewhere?" he asked nonchalantly, as she sat on the edge of the bed, pulling socks and a pair of white sneakers onto her feet.

"We might as well head to the office and get busy researching whatever you had in mind when you were looking for a computer."

He stood up slowly, studying her across the small space of the bedroom. Had their lovemaking had no impact on her? Had it done what she'd hoped and cured her attraction to him? She ran a shaking hand over her hair, and he hid his smile. That unconscious gesture gave him all the assurance he needed. She was just as affected as he was.

"Stay in this room, and don't open the door for anyone," he warned before pointing to the gun on the nightstand. "If you need it, use it."

She paled at the idea of using the gun, and he brushed a hand across her cheek as he passed her on his way to the shower. As an added precaution, he left the door wide open so he could hear any commotion.

He wasn't sure why he'd expected her to do what he said or why he was surprised to find the bedroom empty when he came out of the shower. His pistol was still where he'd left it, his bag lay on the bed, and the smell of coffee wafted down the hall. He sighed heavily as he pulled on his clothes. Didn't the woman ever just relax? At work she was as busy and efficient as a little bee, but he'd assumed at home she'd be different. Or did she think she was on the clock? The idea bothered him more than he cared to admit, when he thought of it in connection with what they'd just done. He ran a hand through his hair, scolding himself for the thought. He couldn't quite fathom her reaction to his touch being forced or coerced by her need for a job. But what if he was wrong? Had Teddy offered Sidra a certain kind of security he could no longer give? Had she turned to Levi to fill his brother's shoes?

He thrust his hand into the pockets of the pants he'd worn yesterday, and it closed over the coin he'd found beside her. He knew without looking that it was identical to the one he'd found on Teddy's nightstand after the accident. His throat went dry, and he stumbled to the kitchen for a glass of anything to quench his bone-deep thirst.

"I need a drink," he announced as he entered the kitchen, his hand running through his damp hair.

"What do you want? I have milk, juice, or tea."

"Whiskey."

"It's nine o'clock in the morning."

"Yes, it is."

"I'm not giving you whiskey at nine o'clock in the morning."

"Why?"

"It's too early."

"And you don't keep alcohol in the house, right?"

"No." She shrugged. "I've never understood the usefulness in drinking."

"This from a woman with a dozen dolls in fancy dresses and a shelf full of romance novels? How useful are those—unless, of course, the woman uses them to feed her delusions and wishful thinking?"

Her eyes widened with hurt, and he wished he could pull the words back, but it was too late. She drew herself up into the rigid lines he recognized so well.

"I find them quite useful in teaching me exactly the kind of man to avoid in my search for true love," she said. "Obviously, I haven't read as many as I should have."

"Do tell, sweetheart, which kind of man do you feel you have unsuccessfully avoided?"

"The kind that thinks it's possible to drink away every bad or good thing in their lives."

He laughed out loud. "You have no idea just how easy it is to silence those things with a few drinks, Miss Martin."

"And you have no idea how devastating loneliness can be to the soul, Mr. Tanner. But keep going as you've been doing and you'll find out soon enough, I'm sure."

She left the room, leaving him to wonder how they had gone from panting each other's names between her sheets to speaking so formally across her kitchen.

Had their lovemaking had no impact on her after all? Had he been mistaken earlier and it had indeed cured her attraction to him? One thing was sure. It hadn't cured him of the questions that circled his head like vultures waiting to pick him clean.

The slamming of the front door brought him to his feet, and he rushed through the house and out the front door.

****

Sidra stalked down the street toward the stop sign at the corner, ignoring the damp chill of the air and counting off the steps in her head. When she reached twenty-five, her mind had cleared enough to let herself think about all that had happened since she stepped into the elevator last night. How much of her memories were real and how many were just wishful thinking? Was Levi right? Was she delusional to think she was a princess, or anything other than a child no one wanted?

"Sidra!" Levi called. "Wait!"

She picked up her pace, but he easily caught up to her, falling into step beside her.

"Sid, you shouldn't be out here. It's not safe. And it's freezing."

"Leave me alone, Levi. I'm fine."

"No, you aren't." He grabbed her arm, pulling her to a stop. "I'm sorry for what I said."

She shook her head, feeling as if she were choking before the words made it past her lips. "You were right, though. I've always used books, especially romance novels and fairytales, to feel better. The heroine's past never affects her happily-ever-after. I guess I've always hoped that's true in real life, too. That even if no one wanted her, she eventually found the one person who couldn't live without her."

"There's nothing wrong with that," he assured her.

She didn't miss the fact that he didn't assure her he was that person or promise her the past wouldn't destroy her chances of living happily ever after. As reality had a way of doing, it settled on her heavily, suffocating the tiny bud of hope that had blossomed at the idea that her family hadn't willingly left her behind.

She closed her eyes, took a deep steadying breath, and forced herself to remember the girl she had been for the last twenty years. Not a princess, and most definitely not the woman Levi Tanner chose to spend his life with. She was merely his secretary. Nothing more, nothing less.

She opened her eyes to find him looking at her with concern. She gave him the same smile she had given for the last four years. He had always accepted it at face value, but this time he frowned at her and shook his head.

"Don't do that, Sid. Don't try to make it okay. I was an ass, and I deserve your anger."

She would have argued with him, but there was no point. Instead she pulled her arm away from him and retraced her steps back to her house.

****

She was sitting on her sofa when he came through the door, the kitten on her lap and Coda stretched out beside her. She stroked the kitten absently.

"Do you know, I don't actually remember being found?" Her voice was soft, distant, as her fingers ran through the cat's fur. "It's as if Sidra Martin didn't even exist before the night Carlotta picked me up from the police station and took me to the first home. I don't even know how my last name became Martin."

"You remembered being kidnapped."

"Only because that man accosted me. If he hadn't, I might never have remembered anything. And I still don't remember much of anything concrete. We don't even know if it's true."

"Give us a little time, Sidra. We'll put the whole story together and you'll know where you came from."

"And who I am."

"There's no question who you are, Sid. You're the same smart, sweet, beautiful woman I've known the last four years. Nothing can change that."

"I'm afraid you're wrong about that, Levi. I think I'm someone much different than we think, and I'm not sure either of us is ready to know just how different I really am from the Sidra Martin you know."

A chill rushed through him at her words. Was she right? When they found out where she belonged, would he have a place in her life, or would he have to turn her loose and walk away?

Chapter Six

A drizzling rain accompanied them to the office, casting a pall over what had happened between them and making Sidra wonder what in the world she had been thinking when she came on to him like that. She had never done anything even remotely seductive in her life, but something in his eyes when he saw her in nothing but the towel had awakened a response in her. Obviously, that response had pushed every rational thought out of her head and she had acted on some primal level she had never before explored.

Now, however, as she studied his clenched jaw and dark eyes, the rational part of her came back with a vengeance. He hadn't spoken since they left her house. Was he regretting their lovemaking? He had warned her more than enough times to keep her distance, that he didn't want the distraction it would cause, but she had kept on, nearly forcing him to react to her.

So here she was, wishing she could bask in the long-awaited proof of his attraction to her, but frightened she had pushed him beyond his breaking point. What would she do if the only person she could trust turned away from her?

She had spent so many years alone, gone through so many foster homes where she was kept an arm's length from anything resembling love or acceptance. There was no denying those years had left her scarred and uncertain of herself, and she had always doubted she would ever find the kind of connection a family of her own would offer.

The day she met Thaddeus Monroe Tanner, "Teddy" to his friends and family, that had changed. He invited her into his world, welcoming her as if he had known her forever, and offering her an easy, brotherly friendship she had never had with the "brothers" she'd known in foster care.

Despite his objections to hiring her and his decision to keep his distance from her, Levi too had accepted her as one of their own.

She doubted Levi would deny the instant attraction that had flared between them, or that it was the driving force behind his aloofness. Assuming she was more to Teddy than just a friend, he had been bound and determined he wouldn't get in the way of his kid brother. Even after Teddy was gone, Levi had held back, obviously reluctant to step on Teddy's toes.

She wanted to assure him once more that Teddy had never been her lover, but she couldn't bring herself to open a conversation in which he would tell her he regretted making love to her. For just a few more moments, she wanted to believe her future held more of them together, that they would find themselves wrapped in each other's arms sooner rather than later or—worse yet—never.

They passed the square where the Christmas tree's lights glowed dismally against the gray skies and the bright red ribbons on its branches hung in sodden clumps.

Christmas in a nutshell, she thought bitterly.

The thought was immediately followed by the

questions her aversion to the holidays always raised. What was wrong with her? Over the years, she had met a person or two who confessed to disliking the increasing flamboyance and materialism of the holidays, but she had never met anyone who admitted Christmas terrified them. She was the only person she knew with that particular phobia, and it disturbed her more every year. Had she ever greeted the season with the anticipation and joy of a normal child?

"I always hated Christmas." The confession took her by surprise, and she wished she could take it back the minute she heard herself say it.

"It scares you," Levi said matter-of-factly, reminding her how astute he was at reading people.

"Yes, it does."

"Can you remember a time when it didn't?"

She shook her head. "No."

He pulled the car into his parking place and turned toward her.

"Have you ever tried to remember?"

Her throat went dry as she considered it. "I can't."

"But you know it has to do with your time before you were found, don't you?"

"Yes, now, I do."

He took her hand in his as they got out of the car and entered the building. "Come on."

The office Christmas tree greeted them the moment they stepped off the elevator on the second floor. Although her automatic reaction was to do what she did every morning and hurry past, he took her hand and pulled her toward it.

"Look at it," he said softly. "Try to remember a time you weren't frightened."

She stared at the white lights, letting them blur before her eyes and transport her to a sunny winter day when everything was right with her small world.

She came every day to admire the massive Christmas tree that stood in the corner of the castle's grand ballroom. Some of the ornaments were so old and fragile Mama would let no one but Papa hang them. They were ornaments her great-great-grandparents had brought to Medelia from their homeland many, many years ago.

She tried to imagine what would be hidden beneath the evergreen's thick branches on Christmas morning. Would Saint Nicholas leave the doll carriage she'd shown Mama on their last trip to the city? It was almost identical to the white wicker pram Nanny pushed baby Andres in on their walks through the castle grounds.

She smiled down at the doll in her arms. Soon Dolly would be riding across the lawn in a white wicker pram with lace trim and a ruffled white blanket covering her. Sidra was certain of it. She had been a very good little girl this year, and there wasn't any reason Santa wouldn't bring her what she wanted most in the world.

A shiver of anticipation raced through her small frame, and she smiled happily as she lifted her face back to the Christmas tree.

Without warning, a large rough hand covered her mouth, a thick arm came around her waist, and Dolly slipped from her hands as she was lifted off her feet. She kicked her legs wildly and tried to wiggle free, but the pressure of his hand on her mouth increased and she grew dizzy from lack of air. The walls and floors tilted, the mirrored walls of the ballroom reflecting the

Christmas lights and transforming them into a vivid whirl in her panicked mind.

"Mama!" She screamed against his hand. "Papa!"

"If they come, I will kill them," he growled, and she stilled. She could not let this man hurt her parents.

He tightened his grip on her, his arm digging painfully into her ribcage as he strode through the ballroom, down the backstairs, and out the door.

Chapter Seven

"Shhh. I've got you, Sidra. It's okay." Levi's voice brought her back to the present, and she was surprised to find herself held tight against his chest while he murmured comforting words against her hair. "It's okay. I've got you."

A shuddering sob shook her, and she clung to him as she told him what she remembered.

"I was just a little girl, looking at our Christmas tree and dreaming about what Santa would bring me. He came up behind me, picked me up, and walked out of the castle." She tilted her head back to look at him. "I was petrified, and no one even knew I was gone."

The fear and confusion in her voice tore at Levi's heart, and he wanted nothing more than to ease the aching loneliness in her eyes.

He didn't try to stop himself from kissing her. There was no reason to fight it. The need to comfort her was too strong.

He caught her trembling lips with his own, swallowing her low hum of acceptance. Her loneliness, her need, her aching desire to be a part of someone else became his own, and he drank it in. She was his now, whether she knew it or not, and he would never again let her face her pain or fear alone.

He was so lost in the kiss it took a moment for his mind to register the sound of the elevator moving upward. He whirled around, pushing Sidra behind him as he drew his gun and aimed it toward the doors.

"D-d-don't shoot," the gangly, freckle-faced kid cried, his hands clutching a large manila envelope. Every freckle stood out in vibrant contrast to the pallor of his skin, and Levi cursed as he put the gun back in its holster.

"Sorry, kid. What do you want?"

He held out the envelope with hands that shook so badly Levi wondered how he kept his grip on it.

"I-I have a delivery for Sidra Martin," he stammered.

"Who gave it to you?" Levi demanded as Sidra snatched it from his hand and ripped it open.

"Some guy downstairs. He gave me ten dollars to bring it up here."

The office phone began ringing and Sidra hurried toward it, removing the contents of the envelope as she moved.

"Tanner & Tanner Invest—" She stopped before asking shrilly. "Who is this? What do you want?"

She looked down at the paper she'd removed from the envelope, and the color leached from her face. The phone slipped from her hand and she grasped blindly at the edge of the desk, her eyes wide with shock.

Levi bounded across the room, catching her around the waist and sinking to her office chair with her on his lap.

He grabbed the phone. "Who the hell is this?"

Low foreign words filled his ears, hateful and guttural sounding, and obviously aimed at Sidra.

"When I find you, you'll be sorry you ever contacted her," he promised before slamming the phone down.

"He wanted to know if I got the picture." Her eyes were still fixed on the paper in her hand.

"Let me see it, sweetheart," he coaxed, prying the picture from her fingers. He let out a low harsh curse.

The dark-haired woman in the picture had not just been murdered but viciously tortured before being killed. Her body was riddled with wounds, blood smeared across her clothing and limbs. It was a horrible image, made eminently worse by the small blond child who knelt beside her, tiny hands covered with blood.

"Shit!"

He slapped the picture face down on the desk, and when Sidra would have reached for it, he caught her hands in his own. Tears stung his eyes as he brought them to his lips, wishing he had been there for her then. Wishing someone had kept her from touching the poor, tortured woman, wishing someone had kept her from witnessing it at all. No wonder her mind chose not to remember what happened. Why on earth would someone want to remind her of it now?

"Is she okay?" the kid asked from the elevator, reminding Levi of his presence.

"She'll be fine." He looked the boy up and down. "What's your name?"

"Danny Ryan."

"Well, Danny Ryan, I need you to come over here and answer some questions about the man who gave this to you."

"Yes, sir." Fear gleamed in his eyes, but he didn't hesitate to come closer. "I'm sorry I brought it up here, man. I didn't mean to upset her. I didn't even know what it was."

"Who gave it to you?"

"I told you, he was just some man downstairs. I didn't know him. I never even saw him before."

"What did he look like?"

"He was kind of short, and not fat but big. Like a football player. He had no neck."

"Dark hair?"

Danny nodded, and Levi cursed, certain it was the same man who had attacked Sidra last night.

"Yeah. He had black hair and black eyes, and his face was smooth as a baby's butt. He didn't have any face hair at all."

Danny ran a finger over his own budding mustache as he made the last proclamation in disdain. Obviously the kid was proud of the smattering of whiskers on his upper lip.

"He had an accent," he continued. "Must have been foreign or something."

"What did he say?"

" 'Hey, kid, you want to make ten dollars? Run this envelope upstairs there. Give it to no one but Sidra Martin.' "

His fake accent was a dead ringer for Dracula, but it was a far cry from what the man actually sounded like.

"Is he waiting downstairs for you?"

"No, sir, he got in a big black car that was parked at the curb, and it drove away." He shot Sidra another worried glance. "What was the picture of, anyway?"

"Nothing you want to see, believe me."

Danny shrugged. "Can I go now?"

"Yeah, get out of here."

The kid was pressing the elevator button before the

words were out of Levi's mouth. As the doors closed behind him, Levi turned his attention to Sidra, who still sat silent and pale on his lap.

"Do you think that's me in the picture?" she asked pitifully.

"Yes. Do you?"

"Mmm-hmmm." She nodded.

"Do you know the woman?"

"No." She shook her head, reaching for the picture.

"You don't need to see it again." He whisked the picture into the drawer and slammed it shut.

"I might remember something if I look at it long enough." The wounded uncertainty in her voice broke his heart. "How could I forget something that horrible?"

"I told you, the mind protects itself from things it can't handle."

"I don't think it will be able to protect me much longer." She turned toward him. "Someone obviously wants to remind me of what happened."

"They could be trying to warn you away from remembering."

The phone rang and Levi snatched it up before Sidra could. "Listen, you sick son of a—" he growled.

A long pause answered his greeting. "I take that to mean they got to her already." Teddy's voice was somewhat wary.

"Ted?" He leaned back in the chair, shaken to hear Teddy's voice after all these months. He closed his eyes against the memory of those moments when he hadn't been sure he would ever hear it again.

"You sound weird. Is Sid okay?" Teddy demanded.

"Sidra's fine." It was a lie. She was far from fine, but he didn't want to explain it to his brother. Suddenly,

Teddy's greeting hit him square in the eyes, confirming the suspicions he'd had since finding the coin. "What the hell do you mean, 'they got to her already'?"

"If you don't know, it isn't something I can explain over the phone. We need to meet in person."

"She was nearly abducted last night, her house was ransacked, and someone sent her a picture of a gruesome murder. If you know anything about any of that, you'd better start talking right now."

"What? Someone tried to abduct her? Levi, listen to me. You've got to get her away from there as fast as possible." He was quiet for a moment, and Levi knew he was probably running his hand through his hair in frustration. "Bring her here. Mom and Dad left this morning for Annie's. They won't be back for a week."

"Tell me what you know."

"There isn't time, bro. If someone is already trying to get to her, if they've really done what you said, they're not going to stop. They're going to keep on until they succeed."

"Succeed in what, terrifying her?"

"No." Teddy's voice was choked with emotion. "They don't want to scare her, Levi. They want to kill her."

"How do you know this?"

"I'll explain when you get here. It shouldn't take you more than three hours. If you're not here in four, I'm sending out a search party."

The urgency in Teddy's voice convinced Levi he was telling the truth.

"We'll be there," he said, pulling Sidra to her feet as he hung up the phone.

"Where are we going?" Sidra cried as he started for

the elevator, her hand clasped in his.

She sounded terrified, and he wondered if he could get away with telling her only part of what Teddy said.

"Teddy knows something about what's going on, and he'll tell us if we come to him."

"Why would Teddy know anything about this?" she demanded.

"I don't know, Sidra," he said impatiently. "That's what we're going to find out."

His eyes surveyed the sidewalk and street in front of the building for a glimpse of the man who had sent the picture. When he saw no one fitting the description Danny had given them or what he himself remembered from the evening before, he pulled open the door and motioned her outside.

"I don't know how long we'll be gone," he said as he pulled the car out of the parking lot. "I keep a bag in the trunk and have a few things at my mom's. We'll swing by your house and grab your clothes and Coda."

"I can't just leave town!" she cried.

"Why not? You have no family. I'm your boss, so it isn't like you're going to lose your job."

"I have commitments."

"Commitments? What kind of commitments?"

"I told you, I volunteer at the nursing home."

"The nursing home?"

"Quit repeating everything I say!"

"You're a volunteer. That means they can live without you, right?"

"I can't leave without at least speaking to them."

"Fine. Call them." He tossed his phone on her lap.

"No, I have to go there. You have to take me."

"What the hell's going on, Sid?"

She sighed heavily.

"Carlotta Strauss is there." She held up her hand when he opened his mouth to speak. "I know you'd like to question her, but I can't let you. That's why I didn't tell you where she was. She has dementia, and I don't want you to upset her with a bunch of questions she doesn't have the answers to."

"So you think I'd just rush in and bombard an elderly Alzheimer's patient with questions she can't answer?"

"Yes."

"I like to think I have a little more finesse than that," he grumbled.

"I just don't want her badgered."

"Have you ever seen me badger an old woman?"

"No, but I've never seen you draw a gun on a kid getting off the elevator either."

He threw his hands up in the air, and she reached to steady the wheel.

"Levi!"

He grabbed the wheel from her and gave her an angry look.

"I didn't know it was a kid. For all I knew it was the same man who tried to abduct you and ransacked your house."

"Do you think it was the same guy both times?"

"Judging by the description, it was."

"So he knows where I live, where I work. How do you know he isn't following us right now?"

She shot a frightened glance behind them.

"He isn't." Levi had made certain of that. There was no one following them. Maybe Teddy was wrong and the man just wanted to frighten her. If he wanted to kill her, wouldn't he have just waited for them to exit the building?

"Will you take me to see Carlotta?"

"Will you find out if she remembers anything?"

Sidra nodded, and turned to stare out the window. He smoothed his hand over her hair.

"You don't have to push her to remember. Just ask her if she does."

"I know," she said, then admitted, "I'm just not sure I'm ready to hear what she might remember."

He understood how she must feel. Twenty-four hours ago, she had no past she could remember. Today, the past was closing in on her, and it was terrifying.

"Where's the home?"

"Freemont Street."

When he turned at the next traffic light and headed in the direction of the nursing home, she breathed a sigh of relief.

"Thank you."

"No need to thank me. I can tell she means a lot to you."

"She was the closest thing to a relative I had growing up. The main goal of the organization Carlotta worked with was reuniting families. I was the only one in any of the homes I lived in who didn't have a family to be reunited with. The other kids got presents from relatives at Christmas, went on visitation, things that at least gave them hope they had a real home to return to one day." She turned toward him. "Carlotta was the only constant in my life, the only thing that kept me from feeling entirely alone. The least I can do is to try to give her the same thing now."

"She doesn't have a family?"

"She never talked about anyone. We didn't talk much after I aged out of the system, but we exchanged cards during the holidays with little notes about the year. Her card was the one and only Christmas item I bought each year. The last card I got from her was written by a nurse at the nursing home just after her stroke. Carlotta had dictated parts of it, and the nurse filled in the blanks."

"What kind of blanks?"

"Not the kind that answered any of the questions we have." She shrugged as they stopped in front of the nursing home. "Basically, it just told me where she was and why."

"When was that?"

"Two years ago. She's gotten much worse since then. She rarely remembers who I am."

"But you keep going."

"Of course, I do. I can't abandon her now."

The air inside the nursing home was so thick with the odors of floor cleaner and disinfectant it burned his nose and brought tears to his eyes. He barely breathed as they made their way down the hall, but Sidra didn't even seem to notice the smell.

She spoke to several nurses and residents, smiling sweetly as a large, gruff man asked if she'd brought him a milkshake.

"Not today, Mr. Whitley," she answered. "Dr. Johnson wants you to work on your diabetes. Remember?"

"'Course I remember, little lady. I just want a milkshake. You're gonna bring me one next time you come, right?"

"I'll try, Mr. Whitley, but I'll have to talk to the

doctor first."

His eyes narrowed at Levi. "Hey, man, did you bring me a milkshake?"

Levi shook his head, and the man shuffled down the hall, mumbling under his breath as he went.

Glancing at his watch, Levi realized that if they didn't hurry night would fall before they reached Gulfview. He had no desire to try to keep one eye on the road and one eye in the rearview mirror in that circumstance. Too much could happen on a two-lane road after dark, especially between towns that rolled up the carpet as soon as the sun went down.

"We've got to pick up the pace a little, Sid. The longer we're here, the more likely we are to be spotted, and we don't want to lead anyone here who might not have connected you to the place already."

Obviously, that thought hadn't occurred to her, because she paled a bit, before giving him a nod of agreement. Just outside Carlotta's door, she stopped and put a hand on his chest. Earnest brown eyes stared into his.

"I ask the questions," she reminded him. "Got it?"

"Got it."

She pushed open the door, letting her usual bright smile spread over her face. Why had he never noticed until now that it wasn't always as genuine as it seemed? Had he been that busy fighting his attraction to her and fuming about her relationship with Teddy?

"Good afternoon, Mrs. Taylor," she said to the white-haired woman lying in the bed nearest the door. "How are you today?"

She straightened the woman's sheet while the woman stared blankly at the ceiling.

"What the devil are you doing bringing men into my room?"

Levi's gaze moved to the woman sitting in a wheelchair in front of the window. From her close-cut salt-and-pepper curls to her sensible navy blue shoes, she bespoke efficiency and professionalism. A dark blue polyester skirt and striped button-up blouse completed her outfit, and he nearly smiled. Sidra rarely showed up for work in anything other than modest, dark-colored dresses or skirts and blouses, and matching pumps. Until this morning, he had never seen her in jeans or anything remotely casual. He sincerely doubted Carlotta Strauss had ever been the beauty Sidra was, but she was obviously the person who had given Sidra her sense of style and decorum.

"Carlotta, this is Levi. He's a friend who is helping me find out about my parents." Sidra made the introductions as Levi took a step forward, and Carlotta glared at him.

"What do I care? I don't even know who you are." Her harsh, slightly accented voice bespoke years of chain smoking.

"Yes, you do. I'm Sidra."

The woman shook her head. "No, you're not Sidra. Sidra was just a little girl."

"I was a little girl when you met me, but now I'm grown up."

"No." She shook her head again, this time a little more vehemently.

"Do you remember anything about her?" he said, and Sidra turned to glare at him, too. Another trait she must have perfected under Carlotta's tutelage.

"Sit down!" Carlotta growled, her words more

accented than they had been moments before. "I can't stand a man towering over me like that, trying to intimidate me and make me tell him the secret."

"What secret?" he and Sidra asked at the same time. The question earned him another glare.

"You can't scare me!" The old woman cried, raking her fingernails down her arms in agitation. Blood sprang to the surface of her paper-thin skin. "I won't tell you, no matter what you do to me!"

Sidra grabbed a handful of tissues from the table beside Carlotta's bed and knelt in front of the woman. She took the blue-veined hands in her own, and held them on Carlotta's lap with one hand as she gently blotted at the self-inflicted wounds.

"It's all right," she said soothingly, shooting him another angry look. "You don't have to tell us a thing."

The woman pulled her hands free of Sidra's and placed one on each side of Sidra's face. When she spoke, it was in the language he was coming to recognize, if not understand.

Sidra paled and stood to her feet, as the woman turned back to him.

"Run," she said in English, eyes burning with fear. "Run!"

Chapter Eight

Sidra grasped Levi's hand before he could ask any questions. She pulled him from the room without a backward glance at the woman she had known for so long yet, obviously, hadn't known at all.

"What did she say?" he demanded, but she shook her head.

"Not now, Levi."

She wasn't translating Carlotta's warning until they were in the car on their way out of town, and even then she would not repeat it all. She couldn't—it was too horrible for words, too terrifying to consider.

They will torture your lover, pluck out his eyes, and take his tongue. They will stop at nothing to find you, and when they do, you will die. The ties have been broken, and there is no other way.

She shivered at the memory and picked up her pace, nearly running to get through the doors.

Once they were in the car, she slammed the locks into place.

"Go!" she ordered, but he ignored her as he turned to stare at her.

"I'm not going anywhere until you tell me what she said."

"She said they'll stop at nothing to find me and I'll die when they do." She ignored his muttered curse. "Then she said something about the ties being broken and there being no other way."

"What ties?"

"I have no idea."

He slammed the car into reverse and pulled onto the road.

"Did you know she spoke that language?"

"No."

"Maybe that's how you learned it."

"It isn't."

"They won't find you and you won't die."

"Quit it, Levi!" she cried in frustration. "Just quit with the platitudes and assurances. Of course they'll find me. They already have."

"We aren't going to be in town long enough for them to find you again. They won't know to look in Gulfview."

"I'm not going to Gulfview."

"Yes, you are."

"No! I'm not. I'm staying home and you're going to Gulfview. I want you to be as far away from me as possible. There's no reason for you to put your life in danger. And I certainly won't let you put the rest of your family in danger by trying to hide me."

"You're out of your mind if you think I'm leaving you here alone."

She sighed. There was no use arguing with him. She would just have to separate herself from him and make sure her assailants knew he was no longer involved. An opportunity was bound to present itself somewhere between here and Gulfview. She could start over somewhere else, somewhere no one could find her, far enough away that Levi would no longer be in danger.

At her house, she packed her suitcase quickly, making sure she had enough of everything to last until she got to wherever she ended up. She scooped up the kitten and, with one last look around her home, walked outside with Coda at her heels.

"You'll be back before you know it," Levi said, and she rolled her eyes.

"You know, you are even more annoying as an optimist than you are in your naturally pessimistic state," she informed him.

He laughed as she put her suitcase in the back seat of his car and went around the fence to her neighbor's house to return the kitten to the screened porch where it belonged. Coda whined as she left her friend behind and followed Sidra to the mailbox.

She rifled through the small stack of bills and sales flyers she pulled from the mailbox, then looked toward her house, the first place she had ever called her own. She had chosen everything in it. She had turned it into her home. The thought of never returning to it brought tears to her eyes, and she dashed them away.

"Good-bye, little house," she murmured, and stepped back from the mailbox.

"Move!" she heard Levi roar, just as she heard the car speeding toward her. Before she could obey, he tackled her, knocking her to the ground with his large, hard body.

He lay on top of her for a long minute, enough time for her heart to nearly stop as she listened for any proof he was still breathing. Had he been hit? Was he unconscious?

"Levi?" she called, pushing at him. "Levi?"

He rolled off her with a low groan, and they both

sat up. She cringed at the smear of blood across his forehead.

"You're bleeding. Are you hurt?"

"No, just knocked my head against something when we fell." He reached up and touched his head gingerly.

She looked around. Judging by the way they'd landed and the angle he'd tackled her from, she would guess his forehead had hit the corner of the mailbox hard and fast.

"Are you sure you're okay?" she asked him.

"Yes. What about you?"

"I'm fine." She was already feeling a twinge or two here and there, and tomorrow she might hurt like the dickens. But it was nothing to worry about. Anyone tackled by a man Levi's size would be sore.

He was on his feet, helping her up, holding her close, his breath hot and heavy on her neck as he pressed his lips to the delicate pulse at the base of her throat. She wrapped her arms around him, noting the pounding of his heart and the fine trembling of his arms. She realized then how frightened he was by their brush with death.

"I'm fine, Levi," she assured him. "I'm fine."

"Thank God," he murmured. "Thank God."

His lips found hers and he kissed her, his hands roaming over her arms, her head, cupping her face as he drank in the taste of her. When he had kissed her thoroughly, he took her arm and escorted her to the car.

"Why the hell didn't you move?" he demanded as he sped down the street. Obviously he was back to normal. "I nearly didn't make it to you in time."

"You could have been killed," she scolded. "What

were you thinking?"

"What do you mean, what was I thinking?" His voice was incredulous. "I was thinking you were about to get run over and I needed to save you."

"He might have swerved before he hit me."

"He wasn't swerving, Sidra. He was aiming right for you. He intended to mow you down."

"The next time something like that happens, you stay out of the way. I won't have your death or injury on my conscience, Levi."

She sounded appropriately cold and professional, almost like her old self. She turned her gaze away from him. She needed to maintain a distance, so that when the time came she could slip away with at least part of her heart.

"So I was supposed to stand there and watch you die?" His voice was as cold as hers, and she knew they were reaching an impasse. "I can't do that."

She hesitated for only a moment, knowing she was about to cross a point of no return, before she swallowed hard and said the one thing she knew would drive him away.

"Why not? You did it to your own brother."

At his sharp intake of breath, she glanced his way, and her heart splintered into a million pieces. His face had gone pale beneath his tan, a nerve ticked in his jaw, and his eyes were bleak with misery as he stared straight ahead, silent and injured.

"Levi, I'm—" She stopped herself. She couldn't apologize or let him see her waver. It was best for both of them that she had driven that wedge between them. She was sorry it hurt him so much, but at least he would live to see another day.

They rode in silence until it became unbearable, and she racked her brain for a topic of conversation that wouldn't lead back to the danger they were in.

"Teddy told me you were engaged when you were younger. Does your fiancée still live in Gulfview?"

"Morgan hasn't been my fiancée in a long time, but yes, she does still live in Gulfview. She's in the Ladies' Auxiliary with my mom. So I run into her every time I go home."

His voice was cold and distant, but she bit back the lingering apology and pushed forward with the conversation she'd started.

"Was your breakup amicable?"

"Yes, and it was a long time ago. We got engaged our senior year of high school. We were young and dumb and thought we had the kind of love that would last forever. It turns out it only lasted until the end of the semester, when she met someone else and I moved away."

"And you've never met anyone else you wanted to marry?"

"No." He glanced toward her. "What about you? Has there ever been anyone you were serious about?"

"No. I've never been very good at long-term relationships. According to the last boy I dated in college, I always had one foot out the door so I could claim to be the first to leave. He thought I had issues from being abandoned as a child. And I thought he was a nosy, interfering crackpot. Of course, if I didn't want to be analyzed, I probably shouldn't have gotten involved with a psych student."

Coda barked softly as if in agreement, and Levi chuckled.

"My parents married right out of high school," he told her. "They've been married forty years, and my younger sister has been married for seven. None of them can figure out what Teddy and I are waiting for."

"Sometimes it takes a while for the right person to come along."

"Yeah," he said softly. "Sometimes it takes a while to accept it when they do."

Before she could respond, Coda barked again, this time louder and more demanding.

"I think she needs to stop. We should get off at the next exit and let her out for a while. Maybe we can find somewhere to eat. I'm famished."

"That sounds like a plan." He looked at the clock on the dash. "Teddy will be sending out the cavalry soon. I'll call him again when we stop."

They parked in front of Tiny's Roadhouse, a small hole-in-the-wall restaurant separated from the gas station and convenience store by an ice cream counter and souvenir shop. They walked Coda in the grassy area on the other side of the parking lot, then returned her to the car, where Sidra cracked the windows so the crisp, cool air could blow through.

She followed Levi inside, and as they walked past the displays of chintzy souvenirs and postcards, Sidra stopped and picked up a small silver spoon. An alligator was engraved in the bowl and a palm tree formed the top of the handle, and she smiled.

"I had one of these," she said softly. "I remember carrying it in my bag from house to house."

"Where did it come from?"

She had a vague recollection of a woman holding the spoon out to her and promising her in a soft, soothing voice that everything was going to turn out fine.

"I don't know. Probably a place just like this." There was no use sharing something that might be a memory and might be nothing more than her imagination. She placed the spoon back on the shelf. "I guess we'd better eat and hit the road."

"Will you order for me?" she asked, once the waitress had placed their drinks on the table and gone away to give them time to look over the menu. "I'll have a cheeseburger."

"Where are you going?"

"The restroom."

He looked around, and she stood up.

"You don't have to keep me safe in the restroom, Levi. I've been using it on my own for a while now."

"Where is it?" he demanded, his eyes narrowing.

"I saw one by the souvenirs."

When it was obvious he was considering following her out and waiting for her, she sighed in exasperation.

"I am going to the restroom, and you are going to stay here and order our food. It will take way too much time for you to follow me, when it's just right on the other side of the door."

"Fine." He grabbed her by the hand before she left. "Straight there and straight back, and keep your eyes open, Sidra. I don't think anyone followed us, but it's always possible."

Her nerves were on edge as she hurried past the bathroom and out the front door of the convenience store. She had to act fast if she intended to leave him behind. She searched the parking lot, dismissing a young couple getting into a car decorated with shaving cream and crepe paper, as well as the white-haired grandparents buckling two small children into their car seats. Her eyes fell on a woman alone, dressed in a charcoal gray pantsuit and black heels. A small, compact purse was clutched to her side, and she walked with a quick, determined gait that told Sidra she wouldn't abide any nonsense but would sympathize with another woman put in a difficult position by a man.

If life had taught her nothing else, it was how to pick the person who would be in her corner and make the best of the situation by befriending them. She grabbed her bag and raised her hand in greeting.

"Excuse me, miss!" she called, grimacing when the woman turned around. "My boss and I were on our way to Tallahassee, but he's in the Roadhouse, drunk as a skunk, and I can't get him out of there. I'd take the car and leave him, but he won't give me the keys."

The woman looked uninterested for a moment, and Sidra pushed on.

"I have to give a huge presentation tomorrow morning at Frasier and Sons. We were supposed to be at the hotel in Orlando long before dark so I could go over my PowerPoint presentation and speech tonight." Her eyes darted around. "The only hotel I see here is shoddy, to say the least, and I just don't feel comfortable staying there. Especially with him."

She added a small shudder that softened the woman's face with sympathy. Seeing her opening, she pressed on.

"If we're not there in time to give the presentation, he'll blame me, and I can't afford to lose my job."

The woman frowned for a second, but in the end,

her face softened and she smiled.

"I'm only going halfway there, but I can give you a ride that far."

Chapter Nine

She climbed into the passenger's seat and the woman backed out of the space. They were pulling out of the parking lot when she looked in the rearview mirror and saw Levi barreling through the roadhouse doors.

"I think your boss just realized you left him." The woman said as a conspiratorial smile spread across her face. "I'm Jess, by the way."

An hour later, Jess exited the interstate and pulled into the parking lot of a strip mall.

"Good luck with the presentation, Sidra," she chirped as Sidra opened the door.

"Thank you so much, Jess. You have no idea how much this means to me."

Headlights illuminated the inside of the car, and Jess looked in the rearview mirror.

"You know, your boss drives pretty good for a drunk guy," she said with a grin.

Sidra's stomach dropped.

"What do you mean?"

"He's been on our tail since we got on the highway."

Sidra tried to cover her fear with a sheepish smile.

"I'm sorry I lied to you. I was afraid you wouldn't buy how much I wanted to get rid of him if I just said it outright."

Jess grinned and dismissed Sidra's apology with a wave of her hand.

"No problem. I enjoyed the company, and the thrill of trying to lose him. It kept my mind occupied."

Sidra glanced around them as she stepped out of the car. Levi's dark blue SUV was nowhere in sight. The lights shining on them belonged to a silver luxury car incongruously parked in front of a darkened cash advance store and a pizza parlor.

"Are you sure you saw him?"

"Of course, he's parked right behind us." Worry creased her smooth brow. "Isn't he?"

Sidra felt herself pale as she stared at the tinted windows of the silver car. She was tempted to get back in Jess's car and demand the woman drive, but she couldn't do it. She couldn't risk Jess getting hurt in whatever was about to happen.

"Oh, yes, there he is," she lied, her voice shakier than she would have liked. "Thanks for the ride."

"Will you be okay with him?" Jess asked, as if sensing her nervousness.

"Sure. We're nearly there now. I'll just insist we drive the rest of the way. Thanks again." She shut the car door, praying the woman would pull away, even while she hoped she wouldn't.

Fighting the desire to run as fast and as far as she could she turned away from the unfamiliar car and walked sedately down the sidewalk in the opposite direction.

They will stop at nothing to find you. And when they do, they will kill you.

Carlotta's words whispered through her mind. Why in the world had she left Levi? *They will torture your lover, pluck out his eyes, and take his tongue.* She took a shuddering breath. She had no choice but to leave him. She couldn't let him die, not for her.

The car crept up behind her, slowly trailing her down the sidewalk. Her heart pounded in her chest and a sob escaped her, as she braced herself for whatever was about to happen. Would they shoot her in the back? Abduct her? She sped up, they sped up, she slowed down, they slowed down, until she was ready to scream with anxiety. Finally, she could stand it no more, and she stopped and turned. It was time to face whoever was following her. Although her knees threatened to give way at any moment, she stood her ground as the back passenger-side door opened and a shiny black shoe appeared. She swallowed hard. If this man wanted to kill her out in the open, he could have done that on a number of occasions. He had ransacked her apartment, so there must be something he suspected she had. Something that he needed before he killed her. At least Levi wasn't here. She had made certain he was out of danger. Unless there was more than one of them, she thought. The thought made her waver where she stood. Had someone hung back to take care of him while this man followed her? Were they torturing him at this very moment, demanding he tell them her whereabouts? Would he be killed because he didn't know the answer to their questions?

Heart pounding, she waited for the dark brawny man who tried to kidnap her to appear. He didn't materialize, however, and the man who stepped from the car was the farthest thing removed from him she could imagine. Tall and blond, with chiseled bronzed features and a lean athletic build, he looked far too noble and debonair to be a kidnapper of women. Was he the mastermind? The one who sent the other to do his bidding?

He stopped a few feet away from her, bending at his waist with a grand flourish of his hand.

"Your Highness," he said in a deeply accented voice. "I am so glad to have found you at last."

Headlights blazed to life behind her, and his gaze darted over her shoulder. Before she could run, he was on top of her, knocking her to the ground as a bullet whizzed past her ear and buried itself in the concrete post beside her.

The man cupped his hand over her mouth to keep her from screaming as the second bullet shattered the window of his car.

A dizzying wave of shock rushed over her, and she fought to maintain control of her mind and body. She couldn't faint. She had no idea if he was friend or foe, but she wasn't willing to take any chances. She had to be alert so she could act on any opportunity to escape.

Any hope of escape died when he pulled a gun and began firing in the direction of the unknown shooter. Gunfire rang in her ears, mixing with the cries of alarm coming from the businesses along the sidewalk.

The shooting stopped, leaving the parking lot in utter silence except for the faint sound of a siren in the distance. Through a billowing wave of darkness, she saw a familiar SUV pull to the curb. Levi flung the door open before he had come to complete stop.

"Get in!" he roared and the man pushed her inside, leaping in behind her as the vehicle surged forward.

The shooter had time to fire only one more time before jumping out of the way of the vehicle intent on mowing him down. The bullet struck the passenger-side mirror, leaving a gaping hole that Sidra couldn't pull her eyes away from. She had come a hair's breadth away from having just such a hole in her.

"Did I injure you, Princessa?" The blond man asked as he turned toward her.

"No," she whispered, his piercing green gaze the last thing she saw as oblivion claimed her and she slumped in her seat.

****

"She's fainted," the man announced in a heavily accented voice.

"Are you sure she's not hurt?" Levi's heart dropped. "She wasn't shot?"

"I'm certain. I had no choice but to knock her down. She would have been killed otherwise."

"Who the hell are you?" He had come into the parking lot just in time to see the man tackle Sidra. It had taken him only seconds to realize the lay of the land and ascertain that this man had saved her life. Although he couldn't think of a reason someone who wanted her dead would save her, he wasn't ready to trust the man, either.

"Philippe Beauchene. I am Princess Sidra's fiancé." At Levi's dubious glare, he continued. "We were promised to one another as infants, and I have been raised knowing she would be my bride."

"I don't think she can say the same," Levi said, darting a glance behind him. When he was certain no one was following, he pulled the SUV onto a narrow, wooded lane.

"We shouldn't stop," Philippe protested. "The assailants could be just behind us."

"They aren't," Levi barked as he got out and opened the back door.

He leaned inside, relieved to see that Sidra appeared to be rousing. He smoothed her hair from her face, watching her closely as her eyes fluttered open.

"What the hell were you thinking, running away like that?" He wanted to sound angry, but his words came out rough with emotion. "You could have been killed."

"I don't want you endangering your life," she told him as he helped her sit up, a steadying hand on her arm. "I thought if I disappeared, they would leave you alone."

"Did you really think I would let you disappear?" How could she think he'd just let her go? Didn't she realize what she meant to him? "Did you think whoever's after you would give up that easily?"

"No, I knew they would find me, but I hoped they would realize you were no longer involved, and you wouldn't be in danger."

"Don't ever do that again," he ordered. "Where you are, I am, and where I am, you are. We're in this together, and if they get to you, it will be through my dead body. Understand?"

Brown eyes stared into his, begging him for something he was unable to give: the assurance that it wouldn't come to that and, if it did, he wouldn't die to save her.

The green-eyed stranger cleared his throat, bringing their attention to him.

"Who are you?" A furrow appeared between her brows as she studied him.

"Philippe Beauchene. I am your—"

"I remember playing with you when we were children." Her voice was filled with awe as she flung her arms around the man's neck, and the uncharacteristic show of affection brought Levi up short.

"You remember him?"

"Yes. He is—"

"Your fiancé?" Levi spit out.

She looked at him as if he'd lost his mind. "I was nothing but a child the last time I saw him. Of course he isn't my fiancé."

"Princess, you may not remember it, but we were betrothed long ago. Our parents tied the bond, and it cannot be broken."

"What are you talking about?" Her voice was frightened, and Levi was reminded of the old woman's words about the ties being broken.

"In our country, each family has a unique woven fabric. It is similar to what the Scottish call tartans. When two families wish to join together, they betroth their children by tying pieces of the fabrics together. The bonds cannot be broken until the wedding is done. Then the two fabrics are sewn together to create a wedding quilt. It is sworn to have powers that bless the union with healthy, numerous offspring."

"Enough!" Levi exclaimed. There would be no union or offspring between Sidra and Philippe Beauchene. Or anyone else, for that matter. He wouldn't stand for it. He closed the back door and climbed into the driver's seat. "We need to get back on the road."

He slammed his door, relieved when the overhead light clicked off, leaving them in darkness. The less

Sidra stared at their passenger the better.

"Where are we going?"

"Sidra and I are going to another town," Levi said, slamming the car into drive. "You, I'm putting out at the next gas station."

"No!" Sidra's voice was sharp and anxious.

Levi's eyes met hers in the rearview mirror.

"You can't leave him unprotected," she said, her eyes luminous in the darkened vehicle. "They'll find him. You saw that picture. They might torture him until he tells them where I am."

"Sidra," he said, but stopped when he saw the plea in her eyes.

"Please." Her fear was thick and tangible, as real as the ground they drove on.

"Fine." He sighed in exasperation and surrender. Turning toward Philippe, he said, "It looks like you'll be coming with us to Gulfview. Sidra will be safe there, and you will do exactly what I tell you to keep her that way. For the moment, start by telling us everything you know about the men who are trying to kill her, and why."

"Have you not told him who you are?" Philippe asked Sidra.

"I have no idea who I am. Three days ago, I was only a woman who remembered nothing of her life before she was found at a rest area on I-95. I have little more information now than I did then, but I'm slowly recalling bits and pieces of what happened."

"My God! You can't be serious!"

"Of course I'm serious," Sidra snapped. "You obviously know who I am, so why don't you tell us?"

He took a deep breath.

"You are Princess Sidra Deleon Maria de Marin of Medelia."

"Medelia?"

"Yes, it is a small but beautiful island in the Mediterranean Sea, near the border between France and Italy." He waved his hands. "Our forefathers escaped the Spanish Inquisition and formed their own colony there. Your roots are deep in Medelia, Princess, and your family has reigned there since their arrival on the island."

"I don't remember it, whether you believe me or not."

"Why wouldn't I believe you? You were barely six years old when you were taken. The kidnapping alone would have been quite traumatic, but the memories of all that happened must have been more than your poor little mind could stand."

"What else happened?" she asked, but Levi knew she was thinking of the picture she had received that morning. At some point in time, she had witnessed a murder, a horrible, torturous murder of someone she might have loved and trusted to keep her safe.

"None of that is important," Philippe told her. "What is important is that you are alive and will be returning home to Medelia. The queen will be overjoyed."

"The queen?" Hope resonated in the quest. "You mean my mother? Did she send you to find me?"

"No. Your parents searched for you for months after your abduction, refusing to give up hope you would be found. They waited by the phone, expecting to receive a ransom note or a demand for something in return for your safety."

"Did they ever receive one?"

He shook his head. "No. They only received one small package. It contained a lock of your hair and a blood-stained tiara. They gave up searching then."

"They thought I was dead?"

"Yes. What else could they think?"

"Do they know you've found me? Do they know I've been found?"

He reached back and took her hand, his voice going soft with sympathy. Levi wished he could shake the feeling that the sympathy wasn't real.

"Ah, my love, I am so sorry to tell you that your parents are no longer alive to know you've been found."

Even if it hurt her, she had to know. Sidra's quick indrawn breath drew Levi's eyes to her. In the rearview mirror, he saw her face register surprise, then pain, as she sank back into the seat and wrapped her arms around herself. His heart broke for her, and he longed to make Philippe stop, but he needed to know everything possible if he was going to keep her safe.

Chapter Ten

Feeling as if she'd been punched in the stomach, Sidra wrapped her arms around her midsection. Her parents were dead, lost to her forever. She squeezed her eyes shut, trying to picture them in her mind.

Mon beau sapin,
Roi des forêts,
Que j'aime ta verdure.

Her father, dark blond hair gleaming in the firelight, motioned her toward him as he sang in a smooth, rich tenor. When Sidra reached him, he handed her the glittering gold star, wrapped his hands around her waist, and placed her on his shoulders.

Her mother, who sat at the piano with baby Andres in a basket at her side, cried out as he grasped Sidra's legs and climbed the ladder with her on his shoulders.

"Be careful, Rupert," she warned, her eyes bright and smiling as she watched them carefully.

Laughing at her mother's dire warnings, he leaned close to the tree, and Sidra pushed the star onto its topmost point. When they stepped down from the ladder, he swung her off his shoulders and spun her around as she laughed with glee.

"I love you, my Sidra," he said softly, placing a kiss on her cheek and setting her back on the ground.

The warm memory faded, and Sidra was alone and cold in Levi's backseat once more. Philippe was studying her closely, while Levi's eyes kept searching her face in the mirror. She wished she could climb over the seat and fit her shivering body against him, but she couldn't do that anymore than she could ignore Philippe's words. She needed to know the answers to the questions rushing through her head.

"How did my parents die?" she asked him.

"Your father died in his sleep a year after your abduction." He raised a hand to silence her. "Though no one really knows what happened to him, everyone has their suspicions. They range from suicide to poison, but no evidence was found to point to either."

"Why would they suspect poison? Who would have done such a thing?"

"I said that's enough for one night," Levi barked out before Philippe could answer.

Although Sidra wanted to argue at his highhandedness, she didn't have the energy to object. She wanted to know everything there was to know, yet the little she had learned in the last few minutes had left her feeling battered and bruised.

Philippe paid Levi no heed at all as he gave the answer to her question.

"Your mother."

She shook her head. "They're wrong."

"How can you possibly know that, darling?" Philippe asked. "You don't even remember the woman."

She had no explanation for the bone-deep certainty that filled her, but she knew beyond a shadow of a doubt the accusation was false. Why would anyone think it was true?

"What about my mother?"

"Your mother was killed in a car accident three years ago. Your brother Andres was with her." He took a breath and continued. "He was killed, as well."

"He was only a baby the last time I saw him. I can't imagine him as a young man." Her voice was so soft and sad it broke Levi's heart. He couldn't stand it anymore. He had to make it stop. Everything else they needed to know could wait until tomorrow. Tonight, she'd had enough.

"Enough!" he choked out when Philippe would have spoken again. "That's enough."

In the silence that ensued, Sidra closed her eyes and thought of the family she had lost so many years ago. In the last few days, she had begun to hope she would meet them again, that they would be happy to see her. Now she would never meet them, never feel her parents' embrace or see her brother as anything more than the tiny baby he'd been twenty years ago.

As if her mind needed something positive to latch onto, she was suddenly consumed by the realization that her parents had loved her. She had lost so many years that she would never be able to make up. She had spent so many years believing she was unloved, maybe even unlovable. And all the while, her parents were grieving over the child that had been ripped from their arms, the child they believed was dead.

Lost in her own thoughts, she nearly didn't notice the change in Levi as they neared his hometown and the brother who had been left broken and bloodied by what Levi considered an unforgivable mistake on his part.

In the passing streetlights, she could see how pale his face had grown. He clutched the steering wheel so tightly his knuckles turned white, and he stared straight ahead.

She leaned forward and rested her hand on his shoulder, squeezing gently. He lifted one hand from the wheel and caressed her fingers before turning his head and placing a gentle kiss there.

She ignored Philippe's disapproving noise. He might say he was her fiancé, but that didn't make it so. Her memories of him only stirred up a rather brotherly affection that paled even to what she felt for Teddy, much less Levi.

Levi turned off the main thoroughfare onto a two-lane street lined with gaily lit historic homes and buildings that housed numerous shops, restaurants, and offices. When they reached a park where a life-sized nativity stood alongside Santa's sleigh and all eight reindeer, he turned again, this time onto a winding residential street with wide, grassy lawns and houses set back from the road a good distance. The paved road became a wide dirt drive that led through a field to a Queen-Anne-style house that looked like it had just popped out of a Christmas card.

A Christmas tree gleamed in the oriel window, and white icicle lights hung from every inch of the outside trim.

"My mother loves Christmas," Levi said apologetically as he opened the car door. "I hope it doesn't disturb you too much."

"No, of course not. I'm used to people celebrating Christmas."

"Christmas disturbs you?" Philippe asked.

"It scares the heck out of me, actually," she tossed over her shoulder as she went to stand beside Levi. It was the first time she had ever said the words aloud to anyone, and she let out a ragged breath of relief.

She turned her attention to Levi, who was staring at the door as if a firing squad waited on the other side. Taking his hand, she pulled him toward the porch, where red ribbon adorned every post. They would face their fears together, whether either of them was ready or not.

****

"How's it goin', bro?" Teddy asked as he stepped out of the shadows of the porch, a metal cane strapped to his left arm and a slow smile spreading across his face.

Tears burned Levi's eyes as he took in Teddy's laughing face and sun-bronzed skin. He looked good, a million times better than he had the last time Levi saw him. That had been the day they carried him out of the hospital to a waiting ambulance. A few hours later, Levi had confirmed with his mother that Teddy had arrived, transported to a facility closer to home for his rehabilitation. He had rarely spoken to her since then, and hadn't spoken to Teddy at all.

Now, after all the months of exile and of nightmares in which he heard nothing but gunshots and Teddy's screams, Levi felt tears prick his eyes to find his brother standing here before him. Still, he held back, unsure of the welcome he would get if he threw his arms around Teddy's neck, certain he would lose the tight hold he had on his emotions if he did so.

Sidra had no such uncertainty. With a cry, she rushed forward, throwing her arms around Teddy as he braced himself for her onslaught. She kissed him on the cheek, twice if Levi was correct, as tears poured from her eyes.

"Good Lord, Sid, it's only been six months, and I've talked to you almost every week." Teddy's laughter belied his protests.

"But look at you!" she sobbed. "You're walking."

"That I am." He grinned at her. "Not as well as I'd like, but I'm doing it."

He turned his attention to Levi and, with a grin, prodded him. "It's a hell of a lot easier for you to come up here than for me to come down there."

With no choice but to respond, Levi went up the steps and wrapped his arms around his brother.

"God, it's good to see you," he said through the lump of tears in his throat.

"It's good to see you, too, brother," Teddy murmured. "I didn't know if you'd ever come home."

"Yeah, I know." He pulled back. He still wouldn't be here if it weren't for the danger to Sidra.

"Mom was heartbroken when you didn't show up for Thanksgiving."

"She knew I wasn't coming."

"We all knew you weren't coming. It didn't make it hurt any less."

"I'm here now."

"So I see. But you aren't here for Mom or me, are you?" Teddy's disapproval ate at him, and Levi's voice showed his annoyance.

"I didn't expect you wanted to see me."

"Yeah, well, you always were good at making assumptions."

Familiar enough with the seemingly innocent turns in their conversation that took it to a more combative level, Sidra stepped between them, her hand on Teddy's arm. It had always been Teddy she chose to soothe, and that bothered Levi now more than it ever had.

"I think we have things to talk about, Ted," she said quietly.

Teddy's face softened, and he gave her an apologetic smile. Levi fought the urge to object to their silent exchange.

"Yeah, Sid, I think we do."

It was hard for him to fathom Teddy being involved in anything that he knew could endanger Sidra, but he couldn't deny what was right in front of him. Teddy knew exactly what was going on, and he'd chosen not to warn anyone until now, when it was nearly too late.

"Who the hell are you?" Teddy said, looking past Sidra to the man standing in the shadows behind her.

"I am Philippe Beauchene, Princess Sidra's betrothed."

"Betrothed?" Teddy choked out, dark gaze swinging from Sidra to Levi and back to Philippe. "So why are you here?"

"I have come to fetch her home." His eyes narrowed. "You don't appear nearly as surprised by my existence as your brother and Her Highness."

"Now that's an impression we share, Phil," Levi drawled.

Teddy let out a weighted sigh.

"I think we'd all better sit down for this," he said, and pulled open the screen door.

Sidra stepped back, her smile fading as she realized what he wasn't saying. Teddy had known, for God knew how long, about her past, about Philippe, about the men who were after her.

"I've got to let Coda out of the car," she said,

turning her back on him.

"I take it they've tried again since I talked to you earlier?" Teddy addressed Levi, but it was Sidra who answered from beside the car.

"They came to my house! They tried to kill me! How could you know I was in danger and not even warn me?"

Teddy cursed under his breath. "I'm sorry, Sid. I should have told you about all of this a long time ago."

"All of what?" Sidra and Levi spoke at the same time.

Coda darted from the car, rushing the porch to greet Teddy as enthusiastically as Sidra had.

"Hey, there, Coda, girl," he said before she dashed back out to the yard.

When she had done her business, she followed Sidra back to the porch as Teddy motioned them all into the living room.

"Have a seat," he said, waving toward the sofa behind them. "This will probably take a while."

Chapter Eleven

Sidra sat on the sofa, and Levi came to stand behind her. She didn't protest when he laid his hand on her shoulder in a protective, comforting hold. Although she was uncertain of what the new physical dimension of their relationship meant for their future, she knew that having him nearby made her feel safe and cared for in a way she never had before. She looked up at him, meeting his dark, furious eyes. Shifting her gaze to Teddy, she felt warmth rush to her face as his eyes moved from her to Levi, realization slowly dawning.

"Tell me what in the hell you've got to do with this," Levi bullied, ignoring the knowing look in his brother's eyes.

"Sit down first. I'm not talking with you hovering over us like the damn angel of death," Teddy said.

"Damn it, Teddy, you'd better start talking."

"Sit down, Levi." Sidra said in a soft, firm voice. "Let him explain."

She was surprised when he sank to the opposite end of the sofa without argument. She smiled to herself as Levi leaned back, his arms folded as if he were unperturbed by the conversation. No one in this room would be fooled by that nonchalant pose, not when his emotions simmered off him in dark, hot waves. It took most of her willpower not to move to his side, but she told herself it was better if she remained where she was so she could watch the interaction of the two brothers as they talked.

Teddy reached for her hand, grasping it in his and staring down at it for a long moment. A slight shifting of Levi's body toward her told her he noticed, even though he said nothing.

"Sid, before I start, I want you to know I never wanted to hurt you. Keeping secrets from you has been one of the hardest things I've ever done. I only did it because it was in your best interest. From what I was told, it was the only way to keep you safe."

"I understand," she murmured, then shook her head ruefully. "No, I don't. You'll have to explain it."

Teddy began his tale in his usual laid-back way, with a sigh and a scrub of his hand across his chin. Moved by the familiar gestures, Sidra felt tears prick her eyes. It was good to have him back, even though she knew a storm was already brewing between him and Levi. They would hash things out as they used to, and everything would be back as it should be soon. Assuring herself of the way things would turn out, she brought her attention back to Teddy.

"Four years ago I was approached by a couple who claimed to be from Medelia, a small, relatively unknown country," he explained. "They told me their cousin, the princess of Medelia, had been kidnapped years before and presumed dead for years. However, they had received some evidence that she could still be alive, and they had come to America in search of her. They were almost certain they had finally tracked her down, but were afraid to approach her for fear she was still in danger from the people who had abducted her. They needed her to remain here in the United States, and they wanted to make sure she was protected until it was safe for her to return home."

Levi leaned forward. "What kind of danger? And from who?"

"They didn't give me a name. If they had, I would already have taken care of the problem." Teddy's voice was harsh and angry. "Maybe they weren't even sure. All they told me was that there were people who stood to lose a lot, should Sidra reappear, and those people would go to any lengths to keep that from happening."

"And now those people have found her." A chill moved over her at Levi's observation.

"It would seem so, yes."

"So why haven't they killed me?" Hysteria edged her voice as she wrapped her arms around her waist. "The man at the train station was close enough to do it."

"I don't know the answer to that, Sidra," Teddy said, her hand still clasped in his. "Your cousins haven't contacted me very frequently. We agreed it would be too easy for someone to track you down if there was too much contact between us. I haven't heard from them in months."

He took a deep breath. "Maybe they tried to contact me and weren't able to, or maybe they haven't. To tell you the truth, I haven't worried about it a whole lot. You never seemed to be in danger, and I knew Levi was there to protect you if you needed it."

She couldn't fault him for not worrying during the last year. He'd been out of commission for months, and even now he wasn't his normal self.

Levi, however, had no such hesitation in finding fault with it. "I can overlook the last few months, Ted, but the last few years? No way. You should have told us long before now."

"You're probably right, but I didn't. You know now."

"You can't contact them?"

"No. The last time I talked to them, they said something about birthdays and marriages, but I had just come back to Gulfview. I was on so many different meds, my brain wasn't working right. I don't know if I didn't understand or just can't remember exactly what they said. All I really understood was that it was nearly time for Sidra to go home."

"Home?" she croaked.

"Medelia is your home, Princess," Philippe reminded her.

"She's a grown woman," Levi argued. "She doesn't have to return to some godforsaken country no one's ever heard of, just because some strangers make arrangements for it. And quit calling her Princess."

"Of course I can't make her return," Philippe agreed easily. "But I think the decision is hers, not yours. And she is our princess, so that is what I shall continue to call her."

She could almost feel Levi's blood boiling.

"You think I don't know that?" he ground out. "I can't force her to stay, any more than you can force her to leave, but I'll be damned if you will railroad her into doing what you say."

"They have her best interests at heart," Teddy attested.

"How do you know that? How do I know it?" Levi leapt to his feet, ignoring Sidra's outstretched hand. "We were a team, damn it, and you decided to do this behind my back?"

Sidra stood to face him, resting a soft, cool hand against his cheek.

"Let's just hear him out," she said, her eyes pleading for his cooperation.

"Fine," he begrudgingly agreed.

When they were both seated again, she turned back to Teddy.

"You didn't just accidentally run into me at school, did you?" Sidra demanded. "You weren't really there to post an ad about a position with Tanner and Tanner. You sought me out and deliberately misled me. How did you know I would take the job?"

"I didn't," he admitted. "I figured if you wouldn't, I'd keep contact with you some other way. Maybe I would have asked you out."

"So you lied to both of us?" Levi barked out, his eyes narrowing at Teddy's teasing grin.

"I had no choice."

"You had no choice?" Levi's voice rose. "You brought her into our lives without telling me we were supposed to be protecting her from someone who wanted to kill her? For four years? Who do you think has been looking after her since you left town? No one! Not me, because I had no idea she was in danger. Do you think I would have let her walk out alone every night if I had known that? My God, Teddy, if I hadn't been watching her out the window the night before last and seen that guy follow her, if I hadn't chased after them, she'd be gone. She might be dead by now."

"I wasn't thinking clearly when I left," Teddy argued. "It took months of therapy to get me to where I am. I couldn't have protected her even if I were there."

"I could have," Levi said quietly.

Teddy nodded. "You're right, I should have told you."

"What now?" Sidra asked in a businesslike voice. Her gaze encompassed both Teddy and Philippe. "You found me. Now what do we do? Is there some way to contact my relatives to find out what our next step should be?"

"Sidra," Levi began. Surely she couldn't be considering listening to these people.

"I have to know, Levi. I can't just ignore it."

"We don't even know it's true." He turned to Teddy. "How do you know you can believe what these people say?"

With slow steps, he crossed the room and pulled a small book from the bookshelf. He placed it on the table in front of Sidra.

"When I told them you didn't seem to remember who you were, they gave me these, hoping this would jog your memory. Maybe Philippe can vouch for their authenticity."

Her hands shook as she opened the album to the first picture.

"Oh, my God," she breathed. "Teddy, I— This is my mother."

Her voice choked as she touched the face of the pretty brunette with laughing, sky-blue eyes and a wide smile. She held a baby in her arms and leaned against Sidra's tall, sandy-haired father, who had one arm around her shoulders and the other around a young girl. In the background, across an expanse of vivid green grass, a large stone castle was visible.

"And that's me." Sidra's fingers moved to the girl.

"You remember them?" Levi asked softly as he

moved nearer to her.

She nodded, unable to speak through her tears.

"Do you remember your life there?" Teddy prodded.

"No."

"Nothing?"

"Only little details that don't amount to much."

She told him just what she had told Levi after her attempted abduction: a little girl's room, her mother, and a carousel on the lawn. She added the memory of her father lifting her up to put the star on the Christmas tree. When she got to the kidnapping, her voice shook and she clasped her hands together tightly in her lap.

"The woman was right," she said. "I never saw them again."

"Is any of what she remembers correct?" The lump in his throat made Levi's voice brusque as he turned to Philippe.

The green eyes glimmered as Philippe dropped to his knees in front of her and brought her hands to his lips. "If I had any doubts you are our princess, your memories have dispelled them."

When Sidra pulled her hands from his, scrubbing them against her jeans, Levi fought a triumphant smile. Sidra had not given in to the man's allure yet. Perhaps she never would.

"Do you remember anything between the time the man took you and when the woman found you?" Teddy asked, and she shook her head. "What about after she found you?"

"After she found me is the only time I really remember. Anything before that is nearly blank. After she found me, I was in and out of foster homes. I was in only one longer than a year, and it wasn't much over that. When I aged out of the system, I went to work as a receptionist at a medical office and started taking some business classes at night. I graduated with a business administration degree the month after I came to work for you."

Levi couldn't help but notice what a condensed version she gave, and he wondered again if her years in foster homes had been difficult. He had no idea why she had been moved so frequently, but it must have been nearly impossible for her to build or maintain bonds with anyone she met.

"Do you still have contact with the woman who found you?"

Apparently Teddy thought he was conducting this entire interview. Levi supposed that wasn't a bad idea, since he'd heard it already. He could think more clearly about her answers and give his attention to watching how she and his brother reacted to each other. It was best to know ahead of time if he was going to have a fight on his hands.

He'd be damned if he'd just stand by and let Teddy have her. He had left her, for God's sake. He had been gone months, although, from what Teddy said, they had apparently had some contact. Still he wasn't going to waltz in here and scoop Sidra up as if she were nothing more than a possession he could do with or without.

In spite of reminding himself that he and Sidra should keep their distance from each other, he placed a hand on her back, letting his fingers run over the ends of her shoulder-length hair as she answered Teddy's questions.

Chapter Twelve

Sidra tossed and turned, trying to get comfortable in the bed Teddy had assigned her. It was obviously the room his mother had set up for her grandchildren to use on overnight stays. Two bookshelves lined with toys, books, and stuffed animals flanked the window. A toy box in the corner overflowed with toys, and a small plastic kitchen across the room boasted a doll-sized high chair and baby stroller.

She wished she could spend the night in Levi's strong protective embrace, but his parents would probably frown upon them sharing the playroom bed, and she had no idea where his room was located. The last thing she wanted to do was end up in Philippe's room.

Philippe had tried to speak with her after Teddy went up to bed, but Levi had interrupted them, showing her to her room and bidding her get a good night's sleep before Philippe could stop him.

She wasn't sure if she wanted to hear what Philippe had to say. Part of her longed to know the full truth of what had happened to her, and why. The other part of her wanted to run as fast and as far from it as she could.

She had spent her childhood sleeping in strange beds, praying she would one day find the place she belonged. Desperate to believe that happily ever after could exist and dreams could come true, she devoured fairy tales and romance novels, fueling both hope and heartache as the years passed with no answer to her silent pleas. Now, here she was about to find the family she had dreamed of, the place she belonged, and she wanted to run away.

A soft knock interrupted her reverie, but before she could answer Levi opened the door. He crossed the room without a word and came into bed beside her, pulling her back against his front and wrapping his arms around her.

"Sleep," he whispered, kissing her softly on the ear. His breath ruffled her hair, and she sighed in contentment.

Within minutes, her eyes shut and she began to dream.

"I don't want this to happen, Gabriel." Her mother's voice was hushed and agitated.

"Jeanne, there is nothing we can do. It must happen, regardless of what you want."

"How can I allow it? She is my child."

Sidra peeked beneath the carousel horse, watching Gabriel's hand tighten on her mother's arm.

"There is only one way to stop it, Jeanne, and I don't believe you are ready to pay that price."

Her mother paled and jerked her arm out of his grasp.

"I will find a way to keep it from happening," she promised. "The ties must be broken, and I will do what it takes to sever them."

"You will die," he warned. "And your family with you. It is up to you. Will she know pain in the future or death at this tender age?"

Sidra gasped, and he crouched down, his eyes

meeting hers beneath the horse's belly. Eyes gray as the rainy sky bore into hers as his mouth formed a grim smile that bared his straight white teeth.

"Your mama would like to play a game, my sweet," he told her.

"Gabriel, no," her mother hissed, but he lifted his hand and flipped the switch beside him. The lights and music surged to life, and the carousel jerked forward, faster than normal, as Sidra clung to the bar beneath the horse. She tried to stand, but the motion was so fast she found it nearly impossible, and the horse caught her on the shoulder, knocking her down. Tears sprang to her eyes at the jolt of pain and the dizzying effect of the ground rushing past.

Her mother screeched for Gabriel to shut the carousel down, but he simply laughed and leapt onto the platform. He lifted Sidra effortlessly and placed her on the horse as her mother flipped the switch that stopped the wild ride. Without warning, Sidra opened her mouth and vomited on the painted back of the white horse she rode.

"Sidra." Levi shook her shoulder and she opened her eyes, glad to find herself in bed on solid ground, not spinning wildly into oblivion as her cousin laughed like a maniac.

She only realized tears were streaming down her face when Levi brushed his fingers across her wet cheeks.

"Do you want to talk about it?"

She shook her head. She wasn't certain what it meant. It felt like a memory, but perhaps it wasn't. Perhaps it was just a very realistic dream.

He pulled her back down beside him, arms

wrapped around her as she turned toward him.

"I can't believe Teddy knew about me all along and never said a thing." She was more hurt by Teddy's duplicity than she had let on earlier, but now it came out in a rush. "How could he know someone might try to kill me and just go along his merry way? Even if he thought he'd always be there to protect me, there was no guarantee. I mean, look where we ended up, and if you hadn't been there, I'd be dead now."

He was silent as she continued. "And don't even get me started on Philippe. I don't care what was promised in another country, twenty-something years ago. I wouldn't marry him if my life depended on it." She rolled onto her back, throwing an arm over her eyes. "But that's the whole problem, isn't it? We aren't sure exactly what my life is depending on right now. Neither of them told us one darn thing that would explain why someone is trying to kill me."

"Maybe neither of them knows," he offered.

"Philippe has to know. We were obviously close when we were young. He knew me when I was abducted. There has to be some reason behind it. Obviously, it wasn't because the person who took me wanted me. They just wanted me out of Medelia. Permanently, it would seem."

Unable to lie still, she sat on the side of the bed for only a moment before surging to her feet.

"We've talked to both Philippe and Teddy, and we don't know much more than we did when we started out." She began to count on her fingers. "This is what we know. One, I was kidnapped, which we knew yesterday. Two, someone wants to kill me, which also knew yesterday. Three, my entire family is dead, which probably has nothing to do with this. And four, some elusive relatives of mine told Teddy about it years ago, and he kept it a secret from me all this time."

"You forgot five," he said. "You're marrying Philippe."

She rolled her eyes in response, and he chuckled.

****

Levi wanted to grab her, pull her back down to the bed, and make love to her. She wore a long, sleeveless nightgown of a soft pink material that hugged her breasts and waist. Her hair was a tousled mess, but he watched as she pulled a brush through it before disappearing into the bathroom.

He could still feel her in his arms, taste her on his lips, and every fiber of his being wanted more of the sensations she awoke in him. But he couldn't shake the feeling that acting on his attraction was unfair to her, given all that had happened. She was confused and scared, and he didn't think she could possibly be thinking as clearly as usual.

When this was over, if she wanted to move forward, he would be more than willing. Until then, it was best if he kept his distance from her, both physically and emotionally. Neither of them could afford to let emotions distract them from the very real danger she was in.

She stuck her head out of the bathroom, a toothbrush gripped in her hand and her mouth full of toothpaste.

"Where is your room, anyway?" she asked before disappearing once again. She reappeared seconds later and waited for his answer.

"Down the hall, second door to the right. Why?"

"I just don't think I can make love in the playroom."

"Are you planning on making love?"

"Yep." She cocked her head to one side. "How about you?"

Good God, yes, was what he thought. What he said was, "Sid, really, I don't think it's a good idea, with all that's going on."

"Listen, I know you have some asinine idea that I'm in such a fragile state of mind right now that I don't know what I'm doing. Or that I can't be sure what I want. But you're wrong. I know exactly what I'm doing, and I know what I want." She straddled him and leaned her face so close to his they were almost touching. "And you are it."

She kissed him then, a long slow kiss that ate up every thought he had other than the feel of her mouth claiming his. When she pulled away, he followed, and before he knew it, she was wrapped around him as he carried her down the hall to his bedroom.

Much later, she snuggled up against him, her face smoothed of worry for the moment, and her body spent. He kissed her forehead, sighed contentedly, and slept with her in his arms, where he was becoming more and more certain she belonged.

Chapter Thirteen

Dawn was barely turning the sky purple when Sidra tiptoed downstairs, hoping not to wake anyone. She needed a little time alone to think and to plan her next move. The first thing on her list was to research Medelia on the computer she had seen in the living room last night.

She tried not to notice the darkened Christmas tree in the corner or the ceramic Christmas village set up in the large bay window. She focused only on the computer, thankful there was no password needed to gain access.

She searched for Medelia, pulling up several photos of high, rocky shores and white sand beaches. A vague sense of recognition met each one, until at last she clicked on a small thumbnail that linked to a picture of the castle she remembered. A strange sort of homesickness swept through her as she studied the large stone structure perched atop a high hill.

She touched the screen, her hand trembling as it met the cold hard glass. She had known her parents' love there. Was there anyone there who still loved her?

"Do you remember it?" Teddy asked from the doorway, and she spun around to face him, a hand clutched to her chest. He grimaced. "Sorry. I didn't mean to scare you."

"I'm a little jumpier than usual, you know. I

remember it vaguely. In my mind I don't know what's real and what's not."

"Can't Philippe help you decipher that?"

"I don't know." Her gaze wandered back to the screen, and she clicked on another picture. This time, a small village, with barefoot children dancing in the streets, popped up.

"I'm not sure I trust him, Sid. Your relatives didn't mention a fiancé to me, so I have no idea if he's who he says or if it's just a ploy to get close to you. What do you make of his story?"

"I'm not sure. You did say they told you something about marriage and birthdays."

"Yeah, but I don't know if they mentioned that your marriage was already arranged."

"I know that I knew him, but my feelings for him are friendly, almost sisterly, not in any way the feelings I want to have for the man I marry."

"Those are the feelings you have for Levi, aren't they?" His dark eyes bore into hers, and she nodded.

"Yes."

"And he feels it for you."

"I don't know about that. He's overly protective and controlling, but he's the same way with you. So I don't give it much weight."

"No, he is much different with you than he is with anyone else." He shook his head, a bemused smile playing about his mouth. "No wonder he didn't want to hire you. He must have realized his heart was at risk the moment he met you."

She thought of the way their relationship had changed in the last two days. Were those changes purely physical to Levi, or was his heart involved? She didn't have to ask about her own. Her heart had been involved since walking through the door of Tanner and Tanner. A part of it would always belong to Levi, whether he wanted it or not.

"How long have the two of you been sleeping together?"

She wanted to deny it, but the heat that rushed to her face gave her away.

"Not long, huh?" he said with a knowing smile. "Was there ever any hope for me, or were you in love with him from the beginning?"

"You have always been my friend."

"That's what I thought you'd say. Thankfully, that's enough for me. But if I had ever wanted more, before you and Levi, would you have given it to me?"

She shook her head. "I'm sorry. I'm not blind. I know you're a very good-looking man, and I care about you very much. But I've never felt what I feel for Levi."

"No, I'm glad you've been there for him. I've been worried about him."

"Me, too."

"He wouldn't answer the phone or return any calls." He ran a hand over his face. "The family has been really broken up over it. None of them could understand why he chose to turn his back on us."

"He feels responsible for you getting shot."

"Why?"

"He says he hesitated too long."

"He drew down on a twenty-year-old kid who didn't appear to be armed. No one can blame him for not shooting."

"You know Levi. He doesn't see it that way. He

sees it as failing you, letting his emotions get in the way of his job, which was to keep you safe. It's been eating him up for months." Tears sprang to her eyes. "It's been torture to see him in so much pain and not be able to comfort him."

"Although my big brother might think he knows it all, he doesn't. He's not omniscient, and there's no way he could have known that kid had a gun." He sank down in one of the large easy chairs. "It took me a while to figure that out, but once I let myself see it, I knew it wasn't his fault. And his job was never to keep me safe. His job was the same as mine—to do some surveillance on a suspected embezzler and report back to the company owner. Neither of us were prepared to be confronted by the bad guy's lookout."

"You can tell him that all you want, but he can't—or won't—forgive himself."

"Because he thinks he has to be responsible for everyone and everything. He's always thought he could control the world by sheer willpower and superhuman strength." In an exasperated voice, he added, "He's never been able to accept he's just a human."

"I've noticed that." She thought of his assurances that he would protect her, find her assailant, and stop him. With Levi, they weren't just empty platitudes meant to calm her. He truly believed his own words, and he would do what he could to keep her safe and stop the people who were after her. But he was only human, albeit a human who would die trying to save her. The truth of it was like ice water to her veins, and she wrapped her arms around herself, trying to ward off the chill of fear.

Teddy leaned forward, his hands closing over her

upper arms. He'd always been able to read her like a book.

"I know you're scared, Sid, but we aren't going to let anything happen to you."

"Will you promise me something?"

"It depends," he answered warily.

"You owe me a promise for lying to me for the last four years."

"Fine," he grudgingly agreed. "What do you want?"

She pulled his hands into her own and held them tightly.

"Promise me that if it comes down to it, you won't let him die for me."

Teddy paled and shook his head. "I won't promise you that."

"You owe me."

"I owe you, so I'm supposed to let you die? I'm supposed to force my brother to let you die?"

"If that's what it comes to, yes."

"Damn it, Sid, you can't ask that of me. Or him."

"I mean it, Teddy. You and I both know he would die to protect me, and I don't want that." She squeezed his hands. "Promise me."

He hesitated a long moment before finally giving her a curt nod.

"I promise." He placed a quick peck on the cheek before standing up. "I also promise it won't come to that."

"Didn't anyone ever tell you not to make promises you can't keep?"

"Sure they did," he said with a grin. "Right before they taught Levi how to avoid kryptonite. Neither of us learned our lessons very well."

****

Levi woke to an empty bed and a surge of panic as he realized Sidra was gone. He jerked on a pair of jeans and bounded down the stairs, calling her name.

"Sidra!" he called as he rounded the corner into the kitchen, where she stood at the stove, scrambling eggs and frying sausage.

"Good morning!" she said, a smile spreading over her face. "Sit down. Breakfast is almost done."

"I thought you might sleep late this morning," he told her.

"She's been up since before daylight," Teddy said from the breakfast nook.

Levi turned to find Philippe sitting at the table with Teddy, who smiled benevolently at him. Philippe's scowl, on the other hand, encompassed him and Sidra equally.

"She should not be cooking for us," Philippe interjected. "Do neither of you understand who she is?"

Sidra turned, a bowl of eggs in her hand. "I like to cook," she told the man, "especially when there are people to enjoy it with me."

"When we marry, you will not cook." He sniffed disapprovingly as he ran his eyes down the pink chenille robe that covered her nightgown. "And you will not traipse around in your nightclothes."

"For the last time, Philippe, I am not your fiancée, and we will not be marrying."

He leaped up, the palm of his hand slamming down on the tabletop.

Levi and Teddy both surged forward, but to his credit, the man faced them without flinching.

"We will leave for Medelia today," he announced. "You will return to your home, and you will realize and accept the truth."

He waved his hand around the room, encompassing everything in sight and possibly the entire world beyond.

"You do not belong here. These are not your people. This is not your world."

"It's the only world I've ever known."

"It's the only world you remember. That is not the same thing."

She flinched from his words, her eyes meeting Levi's. There was no denying the truth he saw in their liquid depths. She was halfway to leaving. He was losing her already.

"Sidra," he began, but had no idea where to go from there. He couldn't blame her for wanting to know the life she had been snatched away from. She was a princess. What girl wouldn't want to return to that?

"You can't go while someone's after you," Teddy supplied.

Levi breathed a sigh of relief at his brother's words. It was true. They still had no idea who was behind the attacks. The only thing they knew was they were somehow related to Medelia. His eyes met Philippe's cold green ones, taking in the thin lips and chiseled jaw.

"He's right," Levi said. "She's going nowhere while she's still in danger."

"Once she's home, we can keep her safe."

"Yeah, right," he scoffed. "You do realize she's here because of a massive failure to keep her safe there, don't you?"

The thin lips grew even thinner as a hiss of anger escaped them.

"She was kidnapped at six, and it took your country two decades to find her," Levi pressed. "I think the fact that she's survived here for that long is proof positive we're better equipped to keep her safe."

"You have no idea what you're dealing with!"

"No," Levi said, moving toward the man, who took a quick step back. "But you do, don't you? And so far, you haven't been as forthcoming as a loving fiancé should be. At least, that's my opinion. What's yours, bro?"

Teddy had slipped up behind the retreating man, a conspiratorial gleam in his eyes as he spoke so close to Philippe's ear that the man jumped.

"I think you're right, big brother. It's time to make sure we've gotten every bit of information out of him we can get."

"I have no more—" His squeaking was interrupted by Sidra, who came to stand between him and Levi.

"What are you doing?" she demanded, hands on her hips, whiskey eyes flashing at him. "Teaming up to bully him? Did you practice by stealing lunch money from kindergartners? Taking candy from babies?"

She swung around to snag Teddy with her anger, and Levi let his eyes roam over her shapely derriere. She was hot as hell standing there, angry indignation holding her back rigid, hands resting on the curve of her hips. Was this what she would look like standing on the front porch calling for their children?

The thought caught him off guard, blindsiding him with the implications. Had they really come that far? For him to be thinking of towheaded kids running wild in the front yard?

He stepped back, trying to get a grip on his emotions. He couldn't let them distract him from keeping her safe. If there came a time when he was called to make a split-second, life-and-death decision, he wanted to have a clear head. He'd been blinded by jealousy the night Teddy was shot, but he refused to have his vision muddled by emotions again.

"What do you know?" he demanded of Philippe again, ignoring Sidra's grunt of frustration.

"I know nothing more than you do, or at least, no more than your brother," Philippe said.

"Don't look at me," Teddy protested when Levi shot him an angry glare. "All I know is what her cousins told me. She's the princess of Medelia, and she's in danger. They didn't give me any more details than that. They didn't even tell me about him."

"Did you ask them for any more information?"

"Of course I asked for more! I'm not incompetent, Levi. Whether you think I am or not."

"I never said you were incompetent."

"Yeah, I know. You never had to say it."

Levi stared at his brother for a long hard moment as Teddy's words reverberated through his mind. Was he right? Had Levi treated him like he was incompetent? Had Teddy always been the little brother, kept a step or two behind Levi for protection? Some good that had done, Levi thought bitterly, surveying the canes leaning against the wall beside him. When push came to shove, he had failed at being the protector, and his brother would pay for it for the rest of his life.

"Damn it, Levi!" Teddy knocked the canes to the ground. "Quit focusing on these damn things! So I got shot. So you hesitated, not shooting what you thought was an unarmed man. What the hell does it matter now? It's done, and I'm getting better every day. Besides, who ever told you that you had to be my damn protector? Why have you always thought I was incapable of taking care of myself?"

Levi lifted his eyes to Teddy's face, which was red with anger and something else he had never seen on his brother's face. Humiliation. Teddy had always been his little brother, and he had been charged with protecting him for as long as he could remember.

The night before Teddy's first day of kindergarten, their father had sat on the edge of Levi's bed and talked to him about his responsibility as Teddy's older brother.

"Son, you're the big brother, and your mom and I are counting on you to watch out for Teddy," his dad had said earnestly. "You've got to make sure he gets on the bus in the morning and off the bus in the evening. I know he's your little brother and he bugs you here at home, but out there in the world, you're all he's got. You've got to help make sure he's safe."

Eight-year-old Levi had taken the admonishment to heart and had gotten in more than one tussle over the years, if not to protect Teddy then to protect the little sister who followed them. As they got older, they migrated into their expected roles, with Teddy becoming the laidback musician and Levi becoming the hardnosed workaholic. If Teddy had demanded his right to defend himself, would Levi have surrendered it willingly? Levi knew himself too well to say yes. The fact was he had always relished the role he was given. He had loved a good fight, had enjoyed being the hero, the protector, the guy everyone relied on to make things right.

He couldn't lie to Teddy and say he was wrong about the way of things. He couldn't say he hadn't thought Teddy incapable of taking care of himself. He had never considered it at all, actually. He took care of Teddy, so it didn't matter if Teddy could take care of himself. But what thirty-year-old man wanted to be taken care of by his brother? Not Teddy, for sure. He had been grown for a while now, and there was no reason for Levi to still be fighting his battles for him. No reason for Levi to shoulder all the blame for what had happened.

"I'm sorry," Levi managed to say through a throat choked with emotion. "I'm going for a walk."

He strode out the door, paying no heed to Sidra's call or the sound of the ringing telephone. He needed to think, to regroup, to get used to the loosening of the guilt that had kept him in a chokehold for the last year.

Chapter Fourteen

The meadow beyond his parents' yard was still surrounded by the split rail fence he and Teddy had helped their dad build twenty years ago. A swaybacked bay and a black-and-white paint pony his mom had recently rescued from being euthanized grazed nearby, having taken the place of the old gray mare they built the enclosure for. Under the huge live oak in the middle, Butter, the Shetland pony, stood watch. Since they'd fenced it in, the meadow had been home to at least a dozen rescue horses living out their last days in peace and comfort as his mother's beloved pets.

The sun cut through the chill in the air, and the silence of the meadow was broken only by the occasional nicker of the horses or call of a mockingbird. One of the neighbors had a fire going, and the smell took him back to the past, to the days when he and Teddy had roamed this neighborhood on their bikes, staying out until their mother called them home at the end of the day.

He had lived in the city for thirteen years now, and although he rarely missed living here, the past year of exile had been hard on him. He hadn't been exiled by his family, of course. His mother had begged him to come home, but he hadn't been able to bring himself to face them. He had barely been able to face himself.

He was only here now because of Sidra, because

the danger to her had outweighed his need for self-preservation. The thought of losing her, of having to face the rest of his life without her, terrified him. So perhaps self-preservation had still been a driving force behind his return.

From here, he could research her past, try to piece together who wanted her dead and why, without having her within their reach. He wanted to breathe a sigh of relief and tell himself that was the case, but he knew they had been followed at least as far as the strip mall where Philippe had found her. They would have killed her there if Philippe hadn't knocked her to the ground. He owed the man for that even if he couldn't stand him, and every bone in his body burned with jealousy at his supposed relationship with Sidra.

He turned to stare at the house he'd grown up in. When this was over and Sidra was safe, maybe he'd come home to Gulfview for good. The Lawrence house had been for sale for a couple years. Maybe he would buy it. If ever a house was built for a princess, it was the pretty Dutch colonial with its gambrel roof and rose-covered entryway.

He stopped short as he realized once this was over Sidra might well have her own life to return home to, a life that didn't include him. What would he do then?

The faint sound of a car coming up the drive sent a chill up his back, and he turned toward the road as Coda started barking up a storm. A dark Land Rover drove slowly up the road, kicking up less dust than Levi had ever thought possible. He began walking toward the house, picking up his pace as the car pulled into the yard and nearly running as the driver stepped out to open the door behind him.

A tall, thin blonde exited the vehicle and surveyed the yard. Dressed in a rust-colored dress suit and brown high heels, she bore an unmistakable resemblance to Sidra. She barely acknowledged him as he trotted into the yard toward the house, but the man who stepped out the other side was not so oblivious to Levi's presence.

"Sir, might I have a word with you?" Although the man's voice was softer than Philippe's and more refined than Sidra's attacker, the accent was unmistakable.

Levi turned toward him, one eyebrow cocked as he surveyed the smaller, mustached man.

"How can I help you?"

"We are looking for our niece—" The squeak of the back door opening caught the man's attention, and he stepped past Levi without another word. "Mr. Tanner, it's good to see you again. I am glad to see you greatly recovered from your wounds. We have come to claim our niece and take her home."

"I see you've met my brother Levi," Teddy said coldly.

"Ah, yes, Mr. Levi Tanner. I should have known." The man turned back to Levi with his hand outstretched. "It's a pleasure to meet you."

Levi grasped the man's hand and stared deep into the insipid gray eyes. He'd made a life out of reading people, knowing what they were after, and why. Although this man said he was here for Sidra, the reason why remained to be seen. Something in his gaze told Levi it had less to do with Sidra's wellbeing than he let on.

Before he could decide what to make of the man's cold, blank stare, Sidra appeared on the porch behind

Teddy. She was dressed in a pair of jeans, a bright blue sweater, and white-and-blue sneakers. Her lips were painted a soft pink and her eyes lightly lined and shadowed. She looked like the typical, sexy girl next door rather than a princess.

The man and woman stared at her in stunned silence for what seemed like an eternity before the woman finally snapped out of her shock and moved.

"Sidra!" she exclaimed as she marched around the vehicle, her hands outstretched. "Darling, it's been so long since we've seen you."

She pulled Sidra into her embrace, although Sidra appeared a bit reluctant to allow it.

"Don't you remember us, darling?" the woman asked, pouting a little when Sidra shook her head. "I am Miriam De Leone. Your mother, rest her soul, was my cousin. And this is my husband, Gabriel."

"Of course," she said hoarsely as she stared at him. "I remember you."

"Really?" The woman's voice was sharp as she looked from Sidra to her husband. "You remember Gabriel? How odd. He and I had not been married long before your abduction." Whatever Sidra remembered about him obviously wasn't something she intended to share. Instead, she motioned to the door, saying, "Let's all go inside where we can talk. Between the two of you and Philippe, maybe we can get the whole story instead of bits and pieces that don't really tell us anything."

"Philippe?" Gabriel exclaimed. "He's here? In America?"

"Yes, he's been here for a week or two, but he just found me yesterday." Sidra led them to the table, her eyes searching the kitchen for Philippe, who was nowhere in sight.

"Where is he?" Teddy asked.

"He was right here." She went to the hallway and shouted his name up the stairs, but there was no answer.

Drawing his gun, Levi rushed upstairs, searching each empty room.

"He's not here!" he called down as he pulled the last door shut behind him.

Sidra was rushing out the front door, yelling for him at the top of her lungs. Her words echoed across the yard, and Levi came out to stand beside her on the porch.

Across the yard, the door to the garage where his father kept the tractor and lawn equipment stood open, and he pointed toward it.

"I'll check the garage. You stay here."

He didn't know why he expected her to listen to him. She might be an efficient, dutiful secretary, but she was the most hardheaded woman he knew. He wasn't really surprised when she trotted along behind him, so close she was nearly stepping on his heels as he ran toward the garage.

The interior of the garage was dark and smelled of diesel fuel and engine oil. He flipped on the light, illuminating the interior, and quickly ascertained there was no one inside.

"He has to be here somewhere," Sidra insisted as they walked back out. "Doesn't he?"

"I don't know, Sid." He pushed the door shut behind them. As he turned, the sun glinted off a small metal object, and he bent to scoop the coin up from the ground.

He held it up for Sidra to see. "Either your

boyfriend was out here, or someone else from Medelia was."

"It has to have been Philippe, but where could he be now?" She sounded genuinely worried, even when she added, "He is not my boyfriend."

"Did you find him?" Teddy called from the porch.

"No." Levi started toward the house, grabbing Sidra's arm and pulling her with him. "He's vanished into thin air."

"He could be lost in the woods, or hurt. What if he's injured and can't call for us?" She tried to dig in her heels, but he kept moving.

"He isn't."

"How could you know that?"

"Believe me, Sid. I can almost guarantee you that man did not go traipsing off into the woods by himself. I'd be surprised if he actually made it to the shed by himself, but I'm willing to give him the benefit of the doubt."

"Do you think he was abducted?"

He took hold of her arms, his eyes burning into hers.

"No, I don't. I know he's gone, but he is a grown man, and there is absolutely no evidence that he left against his will. For all we know, he's taking a walk and will be back later."

"You just said he wouldn't have gone into the woods."

He shrugged. "I could be wrong about that, and downtown isn't far at all. Let's just wait a while and see if he shows up."

She looked as if she wanted to argue, but she remained quiet as he turned back to the house.

"Come on, Sid. It's time to hear what your family has to say."

****

Sidra's heart was racing with worry and dread as she took a seat on the plush loveseat in the Tanners' den. The cozy hominess of the room underscored all she had never had and made her even more aware she was about to find out why. At least she hoped she was.

Levi sat next to her and laid a protective, comforting arm across the back of the seat. His fingers barely grazed her hair, seeming to invite her to snuggle up against him, but she resisted and sat stoically straight in her seat.

Miriam and Gabriel sat side by side on the sofa across from them. Although mere inches separated them, they seemed worlds apart from each other, and Sidra wondered what sort of relationship they had. Something nudged at her conscience: a day she barely remembered, a wedding in an ancient chapel, Miriam dressed in white silk and lace, a veil shadowing brown eyes made red from weeping.

Her mother's soft voice said, "You don't have to do this, Miriam. Rupert will find a way to smooth things over."

"He can't, Jeanne. You know it as well as I do. My fate is sealed." She straightened, dabbed at her eyes, and in a voice shaking with dread said, "Perhaps it won't be so bad. Perhaps we will even come to love each other in time."

"This madness must stop," her mother had hissed. "I will never force Sidra to give herself to a man she doesn't love, a man as cruel and biting as the winter winds."

****

"Sid?" Levi's questioning voice brought her back to the present. "Your cousin asked you a question."

"I'm sorry," she said, offering Gabriel an apologetic smile. "I suppose I was woolgathering for a moment."

Unfazed by her smile or her apology, Gabriel simply stared at her with intense disapproval.

"What do you remember about your life in Medelia?"

"Nothing besides the kidnapping, really," she said. "Philippe confirmed the few things I did remember."

She had no intention of telling him she remembered his conversation with her mother, the dizzying ride on the carousel, or her cousin's dismay at having to marry him.

"Do you remember your parents?"

"Only vaguely. Until I arrived here and Teddy showed me the picture you left with him, I had no idea if the woman I remembered was my mother or someone else."

"That picture was taken only a few weeks before you were kidnapped," Miriam injected. "It was the afternoon of your sixth birthday. Your mother and father had thrown a huge party in the garden, complete with a carousel and—"

"Cotton candy," Sidra finished, as the smell of sweet spun sugar filled her memory.

"Yes, do you remember it?"

She shook her head. "Not really, no."

"After the party, a group of men your mother had hired came to begin decorating for Christmas. There were many strangers at the castle that year. Even though they were all approved by the security detail, there was always speculation that one of them came back for you."

"Philippe said there was never a ransom note."

"I assume he told you about the crown, and the lock of your hair." Gabriel shifted in his seat, turning his body away from his wife and toward Sidra ever so slightly.

"Yes, but he wasn't certain if it contained a note."

"It contained no communication, nor did it need any. Your parents took it as it was obviously meant to be taken."

"They believed I was dead."

"Yes."

"My parents died thinking I was dead?"

"No. At the time your mother died, she had come to believe you were alive."

"What? Why?"

"She received this picture of you in the mail."

He pulled a snapshot from his jacket pocket and placed it on the coffee table. Sidra stared at the image of herself, taken without her knowledge, as she crossed the nursing home parking lot. Her hair was pulled back in its usual Saturday afternoon ponytail, and her face was devoid of makeup. She had no idea when it was taken, although her slightly tanned skin seemed to hint at summer. Her skin crawled at the idea of someone spying on her, watching her while she was completely unaware of it.

She was so spooked it took a moment for the implications of the picture to hit her. She had been going to the nursing home. Whoever was watching her knew she would be there. Did they know Carlotta was there, that she was more to Sidra than an elderly resident of the nursing home where Sidra volunteered? Would they try to make her tell them where Sidra was?

"Who took this?" Levi asked Gabriel.

"I have no idea."

"Bullshit." Levi's voice was deathly quiet, but it filled the space between them with thick distrust.

Gabriel said nothing, only studied him like he was a bug under a microscope. A familiar lump of fear settled in her stomach as those cold eyes turned to her.

"Cut the crap, Gabe," Teddy told him. "Start from the beginning, and tell us exactly what you know."

Gabriel continued to stare at her, ignoring both of the glaring Tanner men. She met his eyes, hoping he couldn't see the nausea that suddenly rolled through her or the uneasiness that followed.

Chapter Fifteen

"You were born the crown princess of Medelia on December twelfth nearly twenty-seven years ago," Gabriel began. "Your full name is Sidra Deleon Maria de Marin. Your mother was Princess Jeanne Maria Batiste de Marin. Your father was Prince Rupert Charles de Marin. You had one brother, Prince Andres Charles de Marin. All are deceased. Your mother's mother, Queen Marie Elizabeth Batiste, is the only immediate member of the royal family still living, besides you."

"My grandmother?"

"Yes, she is growing old and frail, but she is alive and looking forward to meeting you soon."

Sidra could imagine nothing past her recent memories, and after all the years of believing herself abandoned by her family, it was difficult for her to grasp the fact that someone still waited for her to return home.

"You disappeared on December twenty-third, just after your sixth birthday. Medelia is a matriarchal kingdom. The crown is passed down from oldest daughter to oldest daughter. If there are no female offspring, the crown passes to the next linear female. Should you not return to Medelia, or should you have no daughters yourself, the crown will pass to Miriam and then to our daughter, Estella."

Sidra looked toward her cousin, who seemed untouched by the words or the thought of being queen. She held herself regally, her back straight, her face devoid of emotions, and Sidra deduced that Miriam's wedding day wish had not come true. Love had never grown between her and the man she married. Judging from her own experience on the carousel, it wasn't hard to deduce that her mother's dire words about cruelty pertained to Gabriel. Had Miriam walled herself off from the world to protect herself from the man she married?

"And that fact had nothing to do with Sidra's disappearance or the attempts on her life?" Levi asked now, gaining her attention once more.

"Of course not." Gabriel sniffed. "With Queen Marie still alive, it would make no sense at all to kill Sidra."

"But with Sidra out of the picture, it would only be a waiting game for you."

"I have no interest in being queen," Miriam told him, seeming so sincere that Sidra was surprised by Levi's disbelieving scoff.

"Maybe not, but I'm pretty sure Gabe here wouldn't balk at the chance to be king. Would you, Gabe?"

Gabriel simply stared down his nose, making no acknowledgment of Levi's suspicions as he continued talking.

"At the time you disappeared, there were three separate lines of suspicion. First, as my wife explained, was the belief that you were taken by a stranger, someone who had come to the palace to prepare it for your birthday or the approaching holidays, and a ransom note would be forthcoming. The second was that you were stolen away to be held until you were old enough to be forced to marry someone other than Philippe. Someone who would become King of Medelia someday.

"The third was a little-held suspicion that you were taken by one of Medelia's few enemies. During the autumn and winter of your disappearance, tensions were high between our country and several others due to international shipping disputes. However, as tensions died down and problems between us were solved, there was never any proof or reason to believe they had you. When your parents received what they feared was proof of your death, the suspicions did turn to us for a while. For the most part, those suspicions died down as your mother continued breathing."

Sidra cringed at the way he spoke the words, and Levi's hand covered hers.

"This photo was sent to her a year before her death, and she sent us to find someone who would keep you safe until it was time to make it known that you had been found. Because someone was obviously aware of your existence and your whereabouts, we felt we could take no chances by making contact with you or taking you home. We located Mr. Tanner, and he made contact with you. Once we had gathered enough information to ascertain your identity, we returned to Medelia."

"We believed you would be safer in America until the time came for you to be reintroduced as the Crown Princess and for your marriage to Philippe to take place. Once you were married and began to produce daughters, you would be safe enough.

"Your mother feared telling the Queen about the

picture might shock her badly and cause some harm to her health, so she put it off for nearly a year. At some time just before her death, she must have told her, because following Jeanne's death Queen Marie was desperate to believe the girl in the picture truly was our princess. Because your time to marry is nearly upon us, she sent us back to the States to bring you home."

"Marry?"

"You are to marry Philippe on your twenty-seventh birthday, less than a month from now. We will return to Medelia in three days' time, and you will be with us."

"I can't just pick up and leave. I have a life here."

"A life?" Gabriel sniffed. "You work as a secretary in a one-man business that is only slightly better than solvent."

Levi remained still and silent behind her, showing no reaction to the man's barbs or Teddy's quick glance his way.

"You fancy yourself in love with Levi Tanner, but after four years, you are still not sure how he feels about you. He may well abandon you the way he abandoned his own brother." He waved Teddy's anger away. "You have little holding you here, Princess."

"Will she be safe in Medelia?"

Sidra swung her gaze to Levi. "Why are you asking that? I am not leaving."

Gabriel acted as if she hadn't spoken. "Until we know who is behind the attempts on her, we can't guarantee her safety. It will be easy to sniff them out in Medelia, simply because it is a small, close-knit country with few places to hide for long."

"I find that hard to believe, since she was abducted from Medelia to begin with."

"You must understand that we were unaware of any threat." Miriam argued, leaning forward a little. "Sidra was nothing but a child. We could hardly fathom someone would harm her! Even once she was gone, we thought at first she must have wandered off and gotten lost. We were certain we would find her somewhere."

"My wife is right. Since Sidra was taken, security has increased in the palace, as well as elsewhere when the royal family travels."

"We're getting nowhere here," Levi complained. "You've told us a lot of history but nothing that can lead us to the person who is trying to kill her now. And until we find that person, she will not be going anywhere without me."

"You must tell them, Gabriel." Miriam placed a hand on her husband's arm.

"Quiet!" he hissed, staring at her hand in what Sidra feared was disgust.

"It can't be helped." Miriam pulled her hand away. "They must know everything if they are to help us."

"Tell us what you know, Gabe." Levi leaned forward. "Now."

He was silent for so long, Sidra doubted he would answer Levi's command or his wife's plea. Finally, he turned those ice-cold eyes back to her.

She closed her eyes against his frosty glare, but it was there behind her lids, and she wanted to cry out at the memory that followed it.

She wanted to run, but her legs were shaking too badly, her breath frozen in her chest as she huddled on the ground. Her eyes darted to the man lying behind him, his body sprawled on the path as blood pooled around him.

"What the hell are you doing here?" Gabriel growled. His eyes were afire in his pale face, and she scooted back away from him. "Tell no one what you saw here, Sidra. Do you understand me?"

"Yes," she whispered.

"Then, run!"

She did as he told her, scrambling across the yard on her hands and knees before making it to her feet and running the rest of the way home.

"Before Sidra was bound to Philippe Beauchene, she was the fiancée of a distant cousin of her mother and Miriam. Jerald was only a boy when he began exhibiting signs of insanity, and Sidra was barely more than an infant. For a while, the family believed that a serious illness accompanied by a high fever had ravaged his mind and he would recover in time. But as time passed, his mental state only deteriorated more and more."

"Do you believe he might be the person trying to hurt Sidra now?"

"No. Jerald killed himself on the palace grounds before Sidra was abducted. He was seventeen. Rupert betrothed her to Philippe within the week so that the boy's family could not stake a claim on her, and they have been enraged ever since. They are a cruel and ruthless people who wouldn't hesitate to kill a child or anyone else. The photograph Jeanne received was sent by them, along with a promise that Sidra would die very soon."

"You should have told me how much danger she was in," Teddy said. Until now, he had been mostly silent, but his voice burned with anger now. "You let me think I was just acting as a sort of bodyguard in case an enemy found out where she was. You never mentioned that you were certain someone still wanted her dead and knew exactly where to find her."

"We weren't sure how you would react to that. We couldn't have an overzealous protector call attention to her, but we wanted someone who wasn't apathetic regarding her danger. You more than met those requirements without our telling you the whole truth."

"What would have happened to her had Levi and I been taken out of the picture? We couldn't force her to remain at Tanner and Tanner. What if she had quit, or moved away? How was I to really keep her safe with only part of the story?"

"You did an excellent job, Mr. Tanner, and you more than earned your pay. I assure you, we are prepared to compensate you well over the negotiated amount, once Sidra is safely home."

Sidra couldn't escape the gasp of dismay that escaped her. Even when Teddy told her these people had hired him to keep her safe, it hadn't fully hit her that they had paid him to care. A familiar, hollow pit formed in her stomach, and her hand moved to her chest, as if to hold her heart in place. All this time she'd thought his acceptance was real, genuine emotion, but, like it had been in every family she could remember, it had been bought and paid for by someone else.

"It isn't about the money, damn it," Teddy swore. "It's about what could have happened and why we should believe your lies and half-truths this time around."

The woman stood slowly, smoothing her slender, manicured hands over her dress.

"Sidra, darling," she said, "I know this is a lot to

absorb at one time. We will give you some time to ponder what you've learned before making your travel arrangements."

When Sidra just stared at her blankly, she continued. "Gabriel and I will be leaving for Medelia the day after tomorrow. We hope you will be with us when we do."

"I will think about it," Sidra agreed as the woman turned to her husband.

"It's time for us to leave, Gabriel."

He looked ready to argue, but she stared down her regal nose at him until he got to his feet and followed her silently to the door. Sidra wondered about the sudden change in dynamics, but she supposed in every relationship the person with the upper hand was the one who led. And obviously, when it came to getting her to return to Medelia, the two of them had chosen Miriam to do so.

Chapter Sixteen

Sidra stood in the doorway and watched them drive away, grateful they were leaving, but disappointed she still had no idea who was trying to kill her.

She felt Levi come to stand behind her, followed by the soft clip of Teddy's cane on the hardwood floors. She had no desire to speak to either of them. She needed time to think, to come to terms with the thought she couldn't seem to push away. Like every other relationship she could remember, her friendship with Teddy had been bought and paid for.

"Sid," Teddy and Levi said at the same time, but she held up her hand.

"Not now," she said. "I need time to think. I can't talk about any of it now."

"We learned a lot, Sid," Teddy told her.

Her voice was icy. "Yes, we did, didn't we? But there was one thing we didn't learn, Teddy. I never did hear anyone say exactly what the going rate for your friendship is."

His face reddened, and his Adam's apple bobbed up and down before he spoke again.

"It wasn't like that, Sidra," he argued.

"How was it then, Teddy? Explain to me which part of it I have wrong. I was raised by people who were paid to care, so I'm not unfamiliar with the idea. I just never thought it pertained to us."

She couldn't keep the hurt out of her voice or stop the tears that sprang to her eyes. Before either Teddy or Levi could say another word, she growled with frustration and pushed past them. She rushed up the stairs to the playroom, where she plopped on the end of the bed and surveyed the room. It was obvious Betty Tanner doted on her grandchildren. From the three-foot-tall doll house in one corner to the dump truck full of colorful blocks in the other, every item in the room said so. What was it like to have grandparents who loved you? If she went to Medelia, would she find out?

Over the years, she had witnessed a variety of relationships and family dynamics in the homes where she lived. There was one that stood out above all the rest, and it came to her as clearly now as it had when she realized she wanted it.

When she was twelve, she'd lived in a home where the foster parents had biological children. They were kind people who tried to make her feel at ease, included her in family functions, and attempted to help her adjust to a normal life. The endeavor had been unsuccessful, of course, because in less than a year Carlotta showed up at the door and told her to pack for another move. During her time there, though, she had met the family's extended relatives, including the children's grandparents.

Of all the things she envied, that relationship between grandparents and grandchildren was very near the top of the list. From a distance, she watched the relationship, saw the unconditional love, the unending acceptance the grandparents offered, and the joy they all found in each others' presence.

Until a few years ago, she'd had a mother and

brother in Medelia. Even now, she had a grandmother and cousins. How could she pass up the chance to know them? But what if going home cost her Levi?

Home. The word repeated itself in her head, embedded itself in her heart, and she knew the truth. She was going home. Until she did, there was no future for her here. If Levi couldn't accept that, then she would deal with it as best she could.

****

Levi sat at the boy-sized desk in front of his bedroom window. He'd done his homework here, written notes to the girls he liked, and filled out his first job application. Now, here he was mulling over everything he'd learned about Sidra in the last few days and trying to put it all together in some semblance of order in his mind.

So far, the only real conclusion he had come to was that Sidra was leaving him. The knowledge pounded through his head, overriding every other thought and rendering him nearly useless.

He wouldn't let her go to Medelia alone until he knew she was out of danger. If the danger was following her there, so was he. And when the danger had passed, he would do everything in his power to talk her into returning home with him.

Home. For the first time he could remember, the word didn't conjure up thoughts of his parents' home but of his own. His and Sidra's, he corrected, thinking again of the Lawrences' Dutch colonial. He wasn't crazy, and he would never buy a house without her seeing it first, but he was certain she would think it was perfect.

A thought occurred to him suddenly, and he pushed

himself to his feet, stretching his aching back before heading downstairs to find his brother.

He found the canes first, lying against the front porch steps. Panic rushed through him, as his eyes scanned the yard for any sign of Teddy lying on the ground. Had he fallen or been injured in some way? Had someone found them? Had they taken Philippe and now Teddy?

"Teddy!" he yelled, leaping off the porch. "Ted!"

"Where is he?" Sidra called from upstairs. Although she might be mad as hell at the guy, she obviously still cared what happened to him.

"Calm down, dude, I'm right here."

Levi could do nothing but stare as Teddy came around the corner, his arm resting across the neck and back of a fluffy black-and-white alpaca while Coda waddled sedately behind them. They walked slowly, Teddy concentrating to move each leg forward and the animal matching his pace.

"What the hell is that?" Levi asked.

"This is Merilee. She's an alpaca."

"I see she's an alpaca, but what's she doing here?"

"She's a service animal. She helps me exercise, keeps me steady while I walk, and keeps me company when I'm too far up my own ass."

Levi burst out laughing. "She must be a busy girl."

"Yeah, well, I've never known anyone who is perpetually sticking his own head where the sun doesn't shine like you do, brother. Maybe you should think about getting an alpaca, too." He shook his head. "On second thought, the poor thing would probably kick up its heels from exhaustion within a week's time."

The alpaca led Teddy toward the steps, where he

took up his canes.

"You did good, sweetheart," he said, giving her a loving pet on her neck. He grinned at Levi. "Mom was almost as happy as I was when I bought her. You know her love of four-legged beasts of burden. She's going to be heartbroken when we move."

"Are you planning to move?"

"Yeah, I bought the old Morrison farm just outside town."

Merilee looked at him through thick lashes, blinking solemnly.

"Oh, Teddy, look at her!" Sidra exclaimed from behind them, pushing the screen door open and rushing down the steps. "She's gorgeous."

Merilee accepted Sidra's touch, letting her fawn over her for a few minutes before turning her head to look at Teddy with what appeared to be reproach.

Teddy chuckled, "You got it, babe," he said and made some sort of gesture that sent the alpaca trotting toward the meadow where the horses waited.

"I was out there earlier and didn't see her," Levi told him.

"She's trained to stay in the barn until I call for her."

"So I guess your plan to move out to the farm means you aren't coming back to work at Tanner & Tanner," Levi observed, sounding much more disapproving than he felt.

"That's right. I've got a gig up at Mama Jo's, playing piano and singing, which will actually pay the bills while I get the farm up and running."

"So, what? You're going to be a musician-slash-farmer and never leave Gulfview again?"

"Yeah, Levi. That's my plan, and I really don't give a damn what you think about it."

Levi knew by the low growl in Teddy's voice it was no use arguing. Not that he would. How could he, when he couldn't get the idea of moving here out of his own head?

Teddy's cell phone rang, and he grimaced as he pulled it from his pocket.

"Hey, Mom. How's everything going? That's tonight?" He listened for a minute. "Don't worry. We'll clear out so they can do their thing. Yeah, Levi's here with me. He brought Sidra for a visit."

Levi heard his mother's voice rise, and he gave Teddy a thumbs-up.

"Yes, Sidra. It was a spur of the moment kind of thing. No, I don't think she'll be here for Christmas. She's already talking about going home."

Levi's eyes shot to Sidra, who seemed struck by Teddy's words. Teddy shrugged at her, as if to say the words meant nothing, but they all knew differently. They all knew home for Sidra was now a place they had never been, in a world they had never known.

"If I can talk him into staying, I will. Mom, quit crying. I know you're happy Levi's here." He chuckled. "Yeah, I know. We're both here, and you're missing it. Okay, Mom, I'll do my best. Love you, too."

"Is she okay?" Levi asked when he hung up.

"She's crying, but fine. She called to remind me there's a holiday tour of homes tonight. The women's club is setting up in our house and serving coffee and dessert. They'll be here at five, which means we have to find something to do from five until they leave at nine."

"We could take the tour of homes," Levi

suggested, knowing the Lawrence home was always part of it. He would love to see Sidra's reaction to it. He glanced at her. "Can you stand that much Christmas?"

"Do I have any choice?"

"No."

"We'll leave in time to go by and see the farm," Teddy volunteered. "Then we can park in town and start the tour. Afterward, the two of you can come hear me play."

Sidra looked at her watch. "Good, that gives us an hour to search for Philippe."

"Search where?" Levi asked.

"And why?" Teddy shrugged when she shot him an angry glare. "Sorry, but the man gets on my nerves."

"I don't care if you like him or not," she retorted, her voice cold and distant, as she turned to look at Levi. "You go with me, or I go alone. Your choice."

There was no way either of them would let her go alone, and she knew it. She pointed toward the building she and Levi had searched earlier. "We should start there, since we know someone was there. We'll move out from it."

"Does this mean you're not mad at me anymore?" Teddy asked as they followed her across the yard.

"I'm not mad," she told him. "Just hurt, I guess, and disappointed that our relationship isn't what I thought it was."

"Sidra, I care about you. It started out being about the money, but the minute I met you, it became real."

She turned toward them when they reached the edge of the woods. "It's all right, Teddy. I'll survive, and in a few days I'll be back in Medelia."

With that, she turned away and stalked into the

trees behind her.

****

"I don't see anything!" Teddy yelled as they neared the end of the woods.

"Me either!" Levi answered. "Sidra?"

"No." She turned toward the sound of his voice, and stopped in her tracks, the sun temporarily blinding her. A wave of dizziness swamped her, and she stumbled. Dropping to her knees, she fought the horrific memory of murder that surged through her mind.

Blood gushed from Nanny's wounds, running warm and thick through Sidra's small fingers as she grasped the woman's face.

"Get up," she sobbed. "Please, please get up!"

The woman's breath was raspy and weak, her eyes closed and her head listing to the side.

She could hear the man coming closer, his growls of anger as he pushed through the vines and bushes making her shake Nanny, begging her to get up. Suddenly, Nanny's blue eyes flew open and her unfocused gaze locked on Sidra. With the last of her strength, she gripped Sidra's hands tightly.

"Run, Princess!" she hissed. "Run and don't stop!"

Sidra did as she was told, running through the woods away from the woman she loved, fighting to silence her hiccupping sobs of fear and grief. Screams echoed through the forest, and she ran faster, harder, tears pouring down her cheeks. The sound of the gunshot followed her as she burst from the trees onto a clear lawn that led to a large brick building and a parking lot. A man was going through one door and Sidra rushed to the other, pushed it open, and rushed

142

inside, stumbling to the sink, where she began to scrub her hands with soap and water, not stopping even when they turned red and began to sting. She sobbed out her fear as she scrubbed, not realizing someone else had entered until she felt a hand on her shoulder. With a cry, she spun around, coming face to face with the kindest blue eyes she had ever seen.

"Stop, Sidra," the woman said quietly. "You're safe now."

Relief swamped her small form, and she fell into Carlotta's arms with a cry.

She huddled against the tree, trying to get her bearings as the mental picture faded. No wonder her mind had pushed the memory away. She desperately wished she could send it back to wherever it had been, but she couldn't. It was there, in all its gory terror. The fact that Carlotta had been the woman who found her, that there had been no one else who found her and brought her to the police station or anywhere else, barely registered through her shock. But it added one more question to her growing list.

"Sidra!" Levi yelled. "Come on."

She pushed herself to her feet, trembling from head to toe as she moved back up the trail. She saw them as soon as the barn came into sight, both watching impatiently for her return, both realizing her distress the minute their eyes met hers. Levi was the first to reach her, but Teddy was a close second, his usually laughing eyes dark with concern.

"What is it?" Levi demanded. "Did you find him?"

She shook her head, suddenly afraid that if she tried to speak she would burst into tears.

"Did you remember something?" Levi looked into

the trees as she nodded her head. She saw when he realized what memory the forest would have for her. "The murder?"

She took a shuddering breath, and he gathered her close.

"Whose murder, Sid?" Teddy's hand lay on her back.

"A woman whose picture someone sent her. We aren't sure who she was."

She forced the terrible knowledge from her lips.

"I called her Nanny."

Chapter Seventeen

"You look downright festive," Levi teased as Sidra came downstairs an hour later. "How are you feeling?"

Dressed in a red sweater, blue jeans, and boots, she could almost pass for a more willing participant in the holiday festivities.

"Better," she said. "I just wasn't ready for that vivid or violent a memory."

"I wish I could spare you those kinds of memories." He sighed. "Especially when they don't get us any closer to the truth."

The door to the kitchen opened, and Sidra turned, expecting Teddy instead of a pretty, petite brunette in a ruffled red apron adorned with frolicking snowmen.

"Levi, Mrs. Thorpe needs you in the kitch-, oh, hi." The woman stuck her hand out at Sidra. "I'm Morgan Tillman."

She recognized the name immediately as that of Levi's former fiancée, and she smiled as she shook her hand.

"Sidra Martin. I work for Tanner and Tanner."

"Oh!" Morgan's face brightened, although she still looked a bit confused. "Will you be here for Christmas?"

"No, just passing through town on my way home."

"Well, that's nice, then." Morgan smiled and grabbed Levi's hand. "Excuse us. We need his help with some heavy lifting."

"So you met Morgan, I see." Teddy stepped out of the study. "She never has quite accepted the fact that Levi got over her. She's sure if she just tries hard enough she'll win him back."

"She's very pretty."

"Yes, she is."

"Are we ready?" Levi returned, looking like a deer in the headlights.

Morgan was right behind him, surreptitiously applying a new coat of festive red to her lips while his back was turned.

"I wish I could go," she chirped as she slipped the tube of lipstick into her apron pocket, "but I committed to helping here."

"I'm sure the ladies appreciate it, Morgan. You're a great asset to them."

"I'd like to be an asset to y—"

Before she could finish, Levi pulled open the front door and pushed Sidra through it. "Sorry, but we've got to get going."

She pouted prettily as he closed the door in her face.

"Hurry, before she decides she isn't needed here and invites herself to tag along."

"She seems very nice," Sidra said as they got into Levi's SUV.

"She's dangerous."

"Really?"

"No," Teddy answered her with a laugh. "Not unless it's possible to be pampered to death."

"I like sweet, but eating sugar by the spoonfuls just isn't for me," Levi added as he sent his vehicle speeding down the drive like the hounds of hell were after him.

"Morgan just got her third divorce, and after each one she comes looking for Levi. Seems like she can't find anyone who measures up to big bro here."

Levi whipped his head around in surprise, and Sidra couldn't contain her giggle at the double entendre.

"What?" Teddy asked with feigned innocence. "I'm pretty sure Sidra knows you've played the field, and *something* sure made an impression on your little bit of sugar back there."

"Where are we? In eighth grade?" Levi said, his eyes meeting Sidra's in the rearview mirror.

She lost it, laughter overtaking her as she lay across the seat, giggling. She knew the silly pre-adolescent reaction was too much, but she couldn't get hold of herself. For just a minute, she was afraid something had snapped in her mind and she'd gone insane. Then she decided she didn't care. Laughter felt a lot better than the fear that had hounded her for the last few days.

"You're going to pass out if you don't breathe," Teddy told her with a grin, but she just shook her head. He turned back to Levi. "Great, she's completely lost it."

"Yeah, I kind of figured that when she let me kiss her," Levi responded, sounding appropriately despondent.

She felt her face turn red with embarrassment, but she giggled some more, and when Levi finally brought the car to a stop, she lay breathless in the back seat while he and Teddy got out.

The door nearest her head opened, and Levi leaned in, placing a soft kiss on her lips.

"It's good to see you laugh."

She pulled herself upright and climbed out of the car, tears still streaming down her cheeks. Levi shook his head at her, but a smile played at his mouth, and she gave him a quick peck before falling into step behind his brother.

Levi watched her following Teddy toward the ramshackle old house.

"I know it needs some work, but can't you see its potential?" Teddy asked her.

"Of course I can," she said, scanning the house and yard. "It's a beautiful place."

Levi was sorry to say he couldn't see it at all. No one had lived in the house since old man Morrison had been put in a nursing home ten years ago. His daughter had tried to keep it up the first few years, but when he died last year, she'd pretty much given up. Apparently, she'd put it on the market "as is," and Teddy had decided to buy it just like it was.

"Is it livable?" Levi asked, and both Teddy and Sidra glared at him over their shoulders as they kept walking.

"Sure. It just needs a bit of cleaning and decorating."

"I think it needs a damn sight more than that, Ted."

"Yeah, well, beauty is in the eye of the beholder."

"And you've been blinded by Morrison's daughter and the real estate broker. How the hell did they think you were going to take care of this place?"

He wished he could take the words back the minute they were out of his mouth, but it was too late. Teddy turned to him, his eyes dark with anger.

"You are one arrogant son of a bitch," Teddy informed him. "I'm not some damn invalid. Yeah, there will be some things I've got to hire someone to do for a while. I realize I have some limitations at the moment, but I sure as hell don't need you coming here acting like I'm too stupid to know that."

"I'm sorry, man," Levi said. "I worry about—"

"How many times do I have to tell you not to worry about me? Damn it, Levi! You don't always know everything." He turned back to Sidra, who was looking at Levi with unmasked disapproval, and the two of them started toward the house again.

Envy bubbled up inside him, but he strolled along behind them. Their heads were bent close together as Teddy pointed toward the porch, telling Sidra something Levi couldn't make out, and Sidra nodded in agreement. The two of them shared some bond he had never been a part of. Even now, the same day Sidra had been so upset by the idea of Teddy being paid to be her friend, she seemed to have forgiven him. They walked up the steps in tandem, and when Teddy threw open the door, Levi heard her proclaim the interior beautiful with an amazed gasp.

"Look at those floors! Oh, Teddy, this is gorgeous."

"I think so, too. I've been looking for a designer who can come in and make it all just right, but so far, I haven't latched onto anyone." He sighed. "If I don't find someone soon, I'll have to let Mom help, and I just don't know if I could live with her love of all things ruffled."

"We'll find someone after the holidays," she

assured him.

"I thought you'd be gone after the holidays." Teddy was looking at her now, waiting with bated breath for her answer to his unspoken question.

In spite of himself, the same old suspicions rushed through him. He reminded himself it was him Sidra had made love to in the early hours of the morning, and him she had just kissed. He didn't think she was the type to play them off each other. If she was, she had been afforded ample opportunity over the last four years. But she had never done anything that pitted them against each other and had denied his suspicions at every turn.

"Levi, quit glaring and get in here," she said now from a doorway. "You have to see this place."

He stepped into the house and realized immediately that Jennifer Morrison had only let the outside of the house fall into disrepair. The inside gleamed spotlessly and was still fully furnished. It was a house in which time had come to a standstill, and he would guess the year it stopped to be around nineteen-fifty.

"Does it come furnished?" Sidra picked up a figurine in the shape of a Siamese cat.

"Yes."

"All of this stays?" She waved her hand around at the room. "Amazing."

"I'll probably sell quite a bit of it, actually," Teddy admitted. "What do you think?"

"I can't imagine you living here with all these things." She disappeared through the door that led to the kitchen, and Levi stared at his brother.

"What?" Teddy demanded finally. "You want to ask how a cripple like me intends to get all this stuff out of the house?"

"No."

"Then what is your problem? You've done nothing but glare at us since we got here." Teddy's face brightened as the answer dawned on him. "Oh, I see. You're back on your jealousy kick about me and Sidra being lovers."

"Are you?"

"You know what? I'm not even going to answer that." Teddy started toward the kitchen but spun around, anger in every line of his body as he braced a hand on the doorframe. "If you really think Sidra is the kind of woman who would sleep with both of us, you're an idiot who doesn't deserve her."

Teddy stormed into the kitchen, leaving Levi speechless. He was right, of course. Levi knew Sidra better than that. She would never go behind their backs and see both of them, much less make love to them both. It was crazy for him to let jealousy continue to get the best of him when he knew it was unfounded and nonsensical.

With a heavy sigh, he followed them into the kitchen, where Sidra was admiring the gleaming mid-century appliances and kitchen table.

"We've got to get going if we're going to join in on the tour."

Sidra blanched at the reminder but was game enough to agree.

"Let's go, then," she said. "I can't wait to see the homes."

****

Sidra clung to Levi's arm as they traipsed along the sidewalk with their small tour group. She was surprised to realize she was actually enjoying herself despite the abundance of Christmas decorations and holiday cheer inside and outside of each house. The first group of houses had been in the center of town, and they had parked the car and walked. The last two were farther out of town but were close enough together to walk from one to the other after the ride out to them in a hay wagon pulled by a mule. It was waiting to take them back to their cars once they were ready.

Teddy walked at the back of the group, flanked by two women who had come on the tour together, taken one look at Teddy, and made their move. They clung to his arms as the three of them sang Christmas carols, off-key and at the top of their lungs, and Sidra laughed along with everyone else when they improvised their own words for "The Twelve Days of Christmas."

"Watch out, it's rubbing off on you," Levi teased.

A delicious shiver of heat ran through her at the sound of his low voice at her ear. The cool night air made her want to cuddle up against him, and she felt her face warm with the thought of his skin against hers.

She was still trying to get hold of her wayward thoughts when they turned into the Lawrence yard. Her breath caught in her throat. In all her life, she had never seen a prettier house.

Electric candles burned in each window, from the dormer windows on the upper story to the wide picture windows on the front of the house. Even the narrow, floor-length windows on each side of the shiny red door beckoned with light.

She went through the small white archway, heavy with winter roses, and up the sidewalk with everyone else, but in her mind, they faded away and she was alone—hurrying up the path to home, holding her breath, crossing her fingers for Levi to swing open the door and be there waiting for her. She could imagine this as her home, a place to raise children and be a wife. This was a place to put down roots and bloom into the woman she dreamed of being.

She followed the group in and was immediately surrounded by the warmth and coziness of the cottage. A fire crackled happily in the fireplace, where an array of Christmas stockings hung. A Christmas tree stood in the corner, presents strewn under every branch and a star twinkling at the top, reminding her of the memory she'd had of her father.

The smell of fresh-baked sweets filled the air, and she wandered into the kitchen.

"Oh, my," she gasped when her eyes met the beautiful wooden cabinets, gleaming stainless steel appliances, and stained wainscoting.

"Like it?" Levi asked as they left the house a little while later. They were behind the others because she had lingered in the warm, welcoming house longer than was necessary.

"I love it!" she exclaimed. "It's the prettiest house I've ever seen."

"It's for sale."

"It will make someone a wonderful home."

He took her by the arm, forcing her to stop and look at him.

"What about you?" His eyes searched hers. "And me?"

Her mouth fell open, and she stared at him in surprise. "Levi? What do you mean?"

"You know what I mean."

"I—oh—Levi—" She wanted to say yes more than

anything in the world, but she couldn't. Not now. She had to dig up her roots before she could put them down anywhere.

He was completely silent, his eyes dark and cold. "It's okay, Sid. I understand. You don't belong here."

"Levi, no!" Her voice rose, causing Teddy and several others to look in their direction.

"Forget it. It was a stupid idea." He tried to move away, but she stopped him.

She couldn't let him think he had practically proposed and she had thrown it back in his face.

"It wasn't a stupid idea. It was the most wonderful idea I've ever heard, but I can't do it." Tears sprang to her eyes. "Not now, maybe not ever. I have to go home to Medelia, Levi. I have to know my grandmother. I need to know where I'm from."

"But you're not saying no?" He leaned closer, and she lifted her face for his kiss.

"I would never say no to you," she breathed.

"Come on, you two," one of the girls with Teddy yelled. "You can make out later. We're almost done."

"Coming," they both called in unison. With the moment broken, he kissed her softly on the lips, and they turned to follow the group toward the Tanner house.

They were almost there when a figure staggered from the woods to the sidewalk. An older woman at the front let out a screech, and several gasps echoed through the darkness.

"Stay here," Levi commanded as he sprinted to the man, who appeared to be in some sort of distress.

She ignored him, trotting behind him until they could see past the others to the blond head.

"Philippe!" she cried, rushing toward him. Blood dripped from a gash above his rapidly swelling left eye and his lip, and he kept one arm wrapped protectively around his ribs as she wrapped hers around his waist.

"Teddy, you all go ahead inside. Sidra and I will get Philippe in."

Without argument, Teddy led the rest of the group inside.

"What happened?" Levi asked when the others had gone.

"Two men came out of nowhere," Philippe panted.

"Here?" She couldn't control the terror in her voice as her eyes scanned the trees and sidewalk around them.

He shook his head. "I went into town this morning. I was on my way back when they attacked me. I could not see their faces, but they spoke our language. They demanded to know where Sidra was, but I refused to answer. I remember nothing after the initial blows."

"Should we call the police?" Sidra asked.

"No." The men barked out the word in unison.

"They are looking for you, Princess." Philippe grasped her hand in his. "We cannot risk anyone else knowing who you are or that you are here in Gulfview. Not only will it endanger your life but theirs as well."

Chapter Eighteen

They helped him inside and up the stairs to the guest room where he had slept the night before. He fell back on the bed, a low groan escaping him.

"We should take him to the hospital," Sidra cried, but again both men protested. "You could be hurt, Philippe!"

"I am hurt, but not mortally wounded, Princess." He smiled wanly. "Best to let us handle this quietly."

"Levi?" She looked to him for help, but he only shrugged apologetically. "Sorry, Sid, I agree with Philippe."

"Fine," she said in a clipped voice, "then go get a bag of ice for his ribs and a smaller one for his face. A pillowcase, and he'll need some aspirin, too."

Levi stared at her, and she shot him a furious look.

"Go!"

Shock widened his eyes, but he turned and left without protest, coming back a few minutes later with everything she'd requested.

"Take this," she ordered, holding the aspirin and water out to Philippe.

He swallowed it and lay back while she wrapped the large bag of ice in the pillowcase and pressed it to his ribs. Ignoring his sharp gasp of surprise at the sudden chill, she laid pillows around it to hold it in place. She handed him the small bag, which Levi had covered with a washcloth.

"Hold that on your eye."

When she had finished issuing orders, she turned on her heels and headed toward the door.

"Where are you going?" Philippe cried.

"Downstairs. I don't know anything about medical care. If you need anything besides ice and aspirin, you'll need to go to the doctor." Her gaze swung between them. "Levi can take you after he finishes interrogating you."

She paid no attention to their shocked protests as she went down the stairs. She found Teddy in the kitchen with the women from the hayride. The three of them were sampling the sugary confections lined up on a long table, and Morgan Tillman beamed proudly when they described them as the perfect taste of Christmas.

"It's an old family recipe," the woman practically crowed. "I'll bring it with me when I marry, so my in-laws will have a never-ending supply."

She sent a knowing smile Teddy's way, but he only shook his head, murmured something about getting over the past, and moved on to the next batch of goodies.

Sidra backed out of the room before she was noticed, and slipped out the door. She followed the porch around to the back of the house, away from the kitchen and living room. It was quiet and dark on this side of the house, with no Christmas lights, and the laughter and talk from the kitchen was only a soft hum. She settled into a rocking chair, staring into the darkness that shadowed the field and horse stalls. She was used to silence, and the last few days of constant action and noise had exhausted her. Soon enough she would have to go back inside, but for a few minutes she would just sit in the dark and enjoy her solitude.

Not that she could really enjoy it now, knowing that the men had followed her here and had hurt Philippe to get to her. How could she even have enjoyed this evening when he was missing and she had just remembered her nanny's murder?

She still couldn't believe she had forgotten such a horrible occurrence. Maybe her ex-boyfriend was right and there *was* something horribly wrong with her. If that were the case, though, she wouldn't feel so panicked by the thought of Carlotta's warning or the idea of what the men would do to Levi if they felt the need.

She had no choice but to leave and return to Medelia with her cousins. She would never be able to live with herself if something happened to Levi or Teddy, or even Philippe. She could not have their deaths on her conscience. The mere thought of them being tortured and killed made her ill.

"Sidra!" Levi yelled from the front of the house. "Sidra!"

"I'm here," she called.

He came around the corner, illuminated for a moment by the dim glow of the lights behind him. Tears pricked her eyes as she imagined never seeing him again, and she looked down at her hands.

"Are you okay?" he asked, taking a seat in the chair beside her.

"Probably not," she said with a rueful grin. "How about you?"

"Not at all."

She lifted her eyes to him. "I'm scared, Levi. Scared to stay and scared to go."

"I know." He took her hand. "But I'm guessing you're out here for some peace and quiet. So let's just sit here and enjoy it."

"That is a very good idea," she said. She leaned her head back and closed her eyes, savoring the warm comfort of his presence.

****

Levi listened to the familiar sounds of his childhood—the hum of voices coming from the front of the house, the sharp cry of an owl searching for its prey, and the soft nickering of the horses in their stalls.

He absently stroked his thumb over Sidra's hand, enjoying the feel of her soft skin beneath his touch. He couldn't deny the fact that he loved her. The thought of her leaving him was nearly more than he could bear. But the idea of her being killed by the men searching for her was devastating. He could not and would not allow that to happen. If he had to, he would physically place her on that plane back to Medelia. She wouldn't be alone, however. He intended to accompany her. Once she was out of danger, they would focus on where their relationship was going. Right now, his number one priority was keeping her alive.

"I wanted to tell Levi good-bye," he heard Morgan whine.

"Sorry, Morgan, but he's already gone to bed."

"He has not. I saw him come outside."

"Yeah, well, I saw him go back inside. He said he was tired and going to bed."

"With her?" Levi could imagine the pout she gave his brother.

"That is none of your business, Mrs. Floyd."

"Don't call me that, Teddy. You know my marriage to Don Floyd was horrible, and I went back to my maiden name when I divorced him."

Teddy chuckled.

"Yeah, I know. It's amazing how many horrible marriages a gal can have when she's still fawning after the same man. A man, I might add, that she left at the altar."

"We were not at the altar, and you know it."

"Practically," he offered. "If you had gone ahead with the marriage, you could be divorced and over him by now."

"I should slap you for that," she shot back.

"Yeah? Go ahead and try."

She laughed softly.

"Good night, Teddy," she said slowly. "Be sure to tell Levi and his little friend I said good-bye."

"That'll be at the top of my to-do list, Morgan. You be careful on your way home."

The screen door shut behind him, and in a few minutes Levi heard the sound of a car pulling out of the drive.

"You owe me one, bro!" Teddy called from the kitchen window.

"Got it, Ted," he answered. "And thanks!"

"So she left you at the altar?" Sidra asked.

"No. We weren't anywhere near the altar."

"But you were engaged?"

"Yes, but we were going to get through college before we got married. She left for Gainesville, and I went to Atlanta. By December of our freshman year, she had met her first husband. They got married that summer."

"Wow. That had to hurt."

"I guess so, but I don't think it took either of us long to figure out we weren't really getting married." He looked at her. "It was foolish to think we were in love enough to marry if we were willing to be apart for four years. That old saying about absence making the heart grow fonder is a bunch of bull."

"So have you ever come close to marrying anyone else?"

"No. How about you? Any serious relationships in your past?"

"No. I had a boyfriend in high school, but I transferred to another school when I had to move to another home, and we lost touch." She wrapped her arms around herself. "I lived with a guy for a little while in college, but it turned out we weren't as compatible as we thought we'd be. Since then, I've gone out with a few guys, but nothing serious. In the last few years, I haven't seen anyone."

"Are you lonely?"

She shook her head, her arms tightening around her waist. "I have my job, Carlotta and the others at the nursing home, and my books to keep my company."

He was sure she didn't know how hollow her words rang. There was no way any of that filled the very human need for intimacy. He remained silent, however, as he thought of her hungry, passionate responses to their lovemaking.

"I never knew what I was missing until a few days ago." Her voice was so quiet he wouldn't have heard her had there been another noise anywhere around them. "If we had never made love, I would still think that was enough."

"But now?"

"Now I know it isn't."

Before he could respond to her softly spoken admission, she was up from her seat, rushing around the corner of the house. The screen door squeaked open, then closed with a soft thud.

He wanted to run after her, but he held himself still, sensing she needed time to come to terms with her admission and the truth of it. The moment he'd followed her from the office three nights ago, their lives had irrevocably changed, and nothing between them would ever be the same.

****

Sidra knocked on Philippe's door and waited for him to call out to her before she went in and closed it softly behind her. He was sitting up in bed watching television and turned it off when she entered.

"How are your ribs?"

"Sore, but fine."

She sat at the foot of his bed.

"Miriam and Gabriel are returning to Medelia the day after tomorrow. Will you be returning soon as well?"

"I will return only when you do."

She swallowed the lump in her throat. "I will be leaving with them."

"And Levi Tanner? Will he be accompanying you?"

"No," she said quietly. "I will be alone."

"I know it is a frightening prospect to return to a place you don't remember with people you don't know, but Medelia is where you belong."

"How can you be so sure? What if I no longer belong there?"

"It is where you will find your history and face your destiny, my princess. It is where we will marry and where we will raise our children in the bosom of the royal family."

An image of the house she and Levi had visited earlier flitted through her mind, along with his words about her future, but she pushed both away.

"You will not regret leaving this world behind," Philippe assured her. "The people of Medelia need you, and you will never be lonely there. We will marry soon after our arrival, and once we are married and your grandmother has given up the throne, we will begin our reign."

"Why would my grandmother give up the throne?" she asked, trying to ignore the panic that welled within her at his mention of their expected marriage.

"She is old, Sidra, and may want to spend the last few years of her life at her leisure. I'm certain she will step down and allow you to take over once you have settled in."

"How could I be queen when I know nothing of Medelia?"

"You will have me, my love, and I will guide you in every way."

She shivered as she met his icy green gaze. What kind of husband would he be? What kind of king? She shivered as one word whispered through her mind. *Cruel.*

She stood quickly, ready to flee, but he caught her hand in his. "You are mine, Sidra. Regardless of what you feel for Levi Tanner or what you dream of here in

America. Your rightful place is in Medelia, and you were promised to me long ago. I will not rest until you return."

She jerked her hand away from his, curling her fingers into a fist to keep from wiping the feel of his touch from her skin.

"I will return to Medelia, Philippe, but it remains to be seen if I will become queen." She didn't know what made her goad him by adding, "or if you will be my king."

Chapter Nineteen

"I spoke to Gabriel this morning, and he's made the travel arrangements. Our flight leaves Jacksonville at two tomorrow afternoon," Levi informed her when she came into the kitchen the next morning. He was standing in front of the sink, a steaming coffee cup in his hand. "We fly to Paris, where we board another flight to Toulon. From Toulon we can take a ferry or a seaplane to Medelia the next morning."

"We?" He hadn't come to her bed last night, and she hadn't gone to his. Instead, she had fallen asleep as soon as her head hit the pillow, but woke missing his warm masculine body next to hers. Fear he was already letting go had chased her down the stairs, and she breathed a sigh of relief at his words.

"You aren't going there alone, Sid," he said, dark eyes meeting hers, daring her to argue. "I won't stay behind and risk you being hurt."

"Thank you," she breathed as she pressed her trembling lips to his. He gave a hungry groan, and pulled her into his arms.

Desire curled through her, pushed through her veins by the uncertainty of their future, bursting into flame as his hands traced the contours of her body and his mouth left hers to press against the soft pulse at the base of her neck. Through the haze of desire, she felt his hands cup her waist and lift her to the countertop.

He pushed her robe open so his fingers could tease her breast through the soft cotton of her gown. She groaned as his mouth followed his hands, the thin white fabric no barrier against his gentle onslaught.

The sound of Teddy's canes in the hall registered just before the kitchen door opened and he walked in with Philippe just behind him. Although she and Levi separated as the men entered, Sidra knew by Philippe's look of icy disapproval and Teddy's knowing smirk that they were both aware of what had been going on seconds before their entry.

She slid from the counter, Levi's hand still at her waist, and turned to face them. She tightened the belt of her robe as Philippe's eyes roamed over her suggestively.

"You are much like your mother, Princess," Philippe said, disgust thick in his voice. "Before her death, she too found it necessary to whore herself out to a commoner who could never be king. There are some who say that is what cost her life."

Levi said nothing as he stepped toward her, coming up behind so that she fit snugly against him. His arm came around her, holding her there as he spoke in a voice gone deathly quiet.

"Talk to her like that again, and I won't hesitate to beat you to a pulp," he vowed.

They were so engrossed in the little tableau of drama none of them heard the car in the yard until it was too late. At the first shot, Levi took Sidra to the ground, covering her body with his own. When the gunfire stopped, he lifted his head to ascertain Teddy and Philippe's safety. It was quiet only a moment before something crashed through the window behind the table, sending the remainder of the glass raining down on them.

"Run!" Teddy yelled as the car rushed away from the house.

Levi heard the hiss of fire before they stumbled to their feet, pulling and prodding Sidra out the back door. They cleared the porch seconds before one side of the kitchen exploded into flames.

He quickly assured himself that Sidra was frightened but uninjured before he dashed back inside. Luckily the explosion didn't do as much damage as the bad guys had expected, and the fire was confined to the small breakfast nook that jutted off from the main kitchen. He grabbed his mom's mop bucket and began filling it with water, which he tossed on the flames.

Within seconds, Teddy was beside him, a fire extinguisher in his hands, and finished putting out the fire. They both leaned back against the counter, and Teddy shot him a teasing grin.

"Dad's kept an extinguisher behind the back door ever since Mom nearly set the kitchen on fire when she went out to break up a tussle between Annie's boys, got caught up in a water balloon fight, and forgot she was frying chicken."

Levi laughed as he pictured the scene, then sobered as he surveyed the damage the explosion had caused. It was enough to cause concern, but not enough to burn down the house. Obviously destroying the house, or even killing everyone inside, had not been the purpose of the explosive. So what had it been?

His stomach dropped and he rushed out the door, his eyes scanning the yard for the woman he knew wouldn't be there.

"Get in the car," he yelled, breaking into a run to the front yard. He pulled the car around, meeting Teddy halfway around the house. His brother was a whole hell of a lot slower than he had been, but it was still good to have him riding shotgun.

He prayed he would catch the car before it reached the main road, where it would have to turn right or left. Once it did that, he would have no idea which direction to go, and he would have lost her completely.

****

Sidra stared at Philippe in horror as he directed the men to drive faster and farther from the Tanner house.

"You could have killed us!" she cried.

"No, the explosive wasn't that powerful. I only needed time to make our escape. I fear you will never be queen if you continue to play the harlot with your barbaric American."

Her hand connected with his cheek before she could stop it. His eyes turned cold as an ugly red welt spread across his face. He grabbed her arm. For a moment, she feared he would strike her back, but instead he dropped her arm and leaned toward her.

His voice was serious and concerned as he took her hands.

"I have received word that makes me suspect that Miriam and Gabriel were responsible for your abduction as well as for the recent attempts on your life," he said. "I cannot risk you returning with them."

"Levi intended to go with me. He would have kept me safe."

"I have no desire to hurt you, Princess, but you must face the truth. Your family hired Tanner and Tanner, and they have the loyalty of the men you consider your friends. You are only a part of their job, and when the time has come, they will turn you over to your relatives and leave you to fend for yourself."

"That's not true," she said.

"How can you know? Because Levi Tanner saved you from the men who tried to kill you? He was trying to do his job. Because he made love to you? He needed you to trust him, to follow him to Gulfview without question. Haven't you asked yourself how Miriam and Gabriel knew you were there? Teddy claims not to have heard from them in months, yet they contacted him the very day you came to stay in his home. Someone must have told them you were there, and there were only two people who could have done that."

The words were like blows to her heart. She pulled her hands from his and sat back. As if sensing her need for silence, he retreated to his corner of the car and left her to contemplate what he'd said.

She desperately wished she could deny what he claimed, but his words had watered the seeds of doubt planted by her cousin's assurance that Teddy would be compensated for a job well done. She was that job, and the Tanner men had done exactly what Teddy had promised they would. They had kept her safe for the last four years and were now about to see the job to completion. Was Levi's plan to accompany her to Medelia really his way of making sure they delivered the excellent customer service he was so proud of, so the job could be deemed a success?

She shook her head in disbelief. There was no way Levi had made love to her only to ensure she would come to Gulfview. Just last night he had asked her to return with him to the cottage with the rose-covered entrance. There was no reason in the world he would have done that if he didn't care for her.

"Levi couldn't have known about Miriam and Gabriel's involvement in my abduction," she said, turning to Philippe.

"It is natural you should feel that way. You are young and fancy yourself in love with him."

"I want to go back, Philippe. You need to have the driver turn around."

"I can't do that, Princess," he said quietly.

"What? Why?" She felt the color bleed from her face, leaving her chilled. "Take me back to Levi and Teddy. I will return to Medelia with my cousins, and we will make plans there."

"I'm sorry, love, but that isn't going to happen."

****

"Sidra's been kidnapped. Philippe's taken her."

Levi listened to Teddy's call to Gabriel, wondering what the man thought about that fact.

The car carrying Sidra was a black dot ahead of him, obviously heading for open road and the faster speeds of the highway. He had to catch him before he reached it, or he might never do so.

"Where could he be taking her?" He couldn't imagine where Philippe intended to go. Did he intend to take her home to Medelia? Levi prayed that was his intention, but he had a sinking suspicion that Sidra was in more danger now than ever.

"Gabriel and Miriam are on their way. They were already heading to the house, but now they've turned on Sawmill Road and will try to head Philippe off or, at least, get nearer to him than we are."

"Did they have any idea why he took her?"

"They weren't sure, but they think maybe he's going to force her to marry him."

"He can't force her to marry him," Levi assured Teddy and himself. "She is a grown woman, a United States citizen. She can make her own decisions about who she'll marry."

"If he gets her to Medelia, she'll have to. He's her fiancé there, and according to their law she has no choice in the matter."

Up ahead the Land Rover darted out from a side road and came to a stop in front of Philippe's vehicle. The big sedan swerved, lost traction, and spun about before landing in the ditch on its side.

His heart dropped, and he felt physically ill as he rushed toward the upset car. As they neared, the driver lifted himself out of the window, his arm streaked with blood and his face specked with tiny glass cuts. He slid from the car, and Levi waited for Sidra to follow him, but there was no further movement.

"Where is she?" Teddy's voice was sharp and panicked as Levi slammed on the brakes and leapt from the car.

"Sidra!" Her name roared from his lips, and he pounded across the road, desperate to get to her before it was too late. If it wasn't already too late. The thought was enough to make him stumble, but he pushed forward, unwilling to let her stay there, injured, one moment longer.

He threw himself over the car door, peering into the back seat, and his eyes took in what his mind could not comprehend. The car was completely empty.

He turned to the driver, smashing his fist into his face before anyone could stop him. The man staggered backwards, and Levi was on him in an instant, forcing him to the ground and pinning him there with his hand on his throat.

"Where is she?" he demanded, but the man stared at him blankly. "Where the hell is she, damn it?"

The man's eyes were wide with fear, and he shook his head, obviously not understanding Levi's words.

Levi motioned toward Gabriel and Miriam. "One of you get over here now."

He wasn't all that surprised when it was Miriam's high-heeled feet that came into his line of vision.

"Ask him where she is."

She and the man exchanged words.

"He says he doesn't know," she translated. "But I think he's lying."

"Tell him that."

As she spoke again, Levi's hand tightened, and the driver's reddened face turned nearly purple as his eyes rolled in fear.

She spoke again, sharper, angrier, with the authority Levi would expect her to have over a citizen of her country. She might not be queen but she was most certainly royalty, and the man seemed to recognize her authority and the very real danger he was in. He nodded his head, clawing at Levi's hand, and it loosened ever so slightly. He gulped air as Miriam spoke to him again, and he wheezed out an answer to her question.

"What did he say?" Levi asked.

"He said she is in another car and is being taken to the airport in Jacksonville. There is a flight to Paris leaving tonight."

The man continued to babble on, as if unable to

stop now that he had started. Miriam translated without a hint of the emotion the man displayed.

"He says there is an old lady in the trunk of the car they are in. If she is not already dead, she will be before they reach Jacksonville. They kidnapped her three days ago from a nursing facility."

Shocked by the news, Levi lifted his gaze to her, struck by how eyes nearly identical to Sidra's could remain so cold and unaffected by the words she spoke. She arched one delicate eyebrow. "Do you know who she is?"

"Her name is Carlotta Strauss. She was Sidra's caseworker once she entered the foster system."

"We must go!" Gabriel exclaimed. He had been on his cell phone but now motioned wildly. "Leave him be. There's nothing to be gained from him, and we must go at once."

"What is it, Gabriel?" Miriam snapped, grabbing him by the arms. "What has happened?"

"I just spoke with Estella. Philippe Beauchene has been at the castle since Monday. There is no way he is in America."

"Who has Sidra, then?" Levi's gaze shot to the man lying on the ground and he barked out a question for Miriam to interpret.

"Who do you work for?"

The man shrugged helplessly.

"He has to know something," Levi growled. "What does the man look like?"

"Ask him the man's eye color," Gabriel said. "That will tell us if we're dealing with him or not."

"Him who? What haven't you told me?" Levi's eyes swung between Sidra's cousins.

"Ask him!" Gabriel hissed. "We must go!"

"*Quelle couleur yeux a-t-il?*" Miriam demanded.

"*Vert.*"

Levi knew what he meant even before Miriam translated. *Green eyes.*

"Vincente Mateo?" There was no mistaking Miriam's surprise. "He is here?"

"Who the hell is Vincente Mateo?" Levi snapped, meeting her eyes. A chill rushed through him as she answered.

"A man who is a far larger threat to Sidra than anyone else could ever be."

Chapter Twenty

"Take me home, now!" Sidra ordered.

"It is not your home, and I will not take you there."

She turned and grasped the door latch beside her. It clicked uselessly, and panic welled inside her. She beat at the window, but to no avail. There was no escaping as he moved toward her, wrapped an arm around her, and pulled her back against him.

"Let go of me," she said, but he remained silent, letting his arm hook around her neck and tighten slightly. "Let go!"

The arm tightened more and more, until she could barely breathe, and her head spun dizzily.

"Please," she whispered as darkness encroached on her vision.

He loosened his grip just before she lost consciousness, and she slid as far away from him as possible.

"I will never marry you," she spat.

His hand shot out, tangling in her hair to drag her face to his.

"Once you are my queen, you will pay the price for disobedience. Until then, I will enjoy having my men mete it out to your lover. You should have listened to your old friend, Princess. She knows well what horror can be inflicted on the innocent." He leaned forward, so their lips were nearly touching, and in the language of their country he spoke the words that had chilled her heart once before. *"They will torture your lover, pluck out his eyes, and take his tongue."*

"How do you know that?" she cried, fear shooting through her as he pushed her away from him and leaned back against the seat, a smug, hateful smile playing about his mouth. "What did you do to her?"

"Nothing she didn't expect, my love."

Bile rose in her throat, and she shook her head in disbelief.

"She is safe there in the home. You could never have gotten to her."

He chuckled. "Of course I could. After all, poor Mrs. Taylor is a dear old aunt of my mother's. Both women were overjoyed to see me. I believe Mrs. Strauss entertained visitors only moments before I arrived. I heard her speaking to them as I waited in the hall."

"Did you kill her?" Her voice shook with grief and fear, despite her best efforts to control it.

"What do you think?"

"I think you are a hateful coward, afraid of a small, frightened, old woman, and you would have sent someone else to do your dirty work."

His blow sent her head snapping back.

"That is your warning, Princess. Do not make me angry again."

Every fiber of her being trembled with fear, but she forced herself to look him in the eyes. "Do you really think I will marry you now that I know what kind of man you are?"

"Why, yes," he said. "I do believe you will."

He ordered the driver to stop, and when they did,

he pulled her from the car and around to the trunk. The driver opened it, and she stared in horror at the small, bleeding woman confined within. Confused blue eyes were wide above the duct tape that covered her mouth. It was a testament to her dementia that she didn't appear to be afraid at all, only lay there in the trunk as if she thought she might belong there but couldn't remember why.

"Take the tape off her mouth," Sidra pleaded. "Please, I want to speak with her."

He nodded, and the driver jerked it off, taking a layer of thin aged skin with it so that blood trickled over the pale lips and chin.

Sidra turned and yanked the handkerchief from Philippe's pocket. She used it to gently dab the blood from Carlotta's mouth.

"Are you okay?" she asked in their native language.

"Yes, my queen," the woman answered.

"I am not the queen," she said.

"You will be." Her gaze fell on Philippe. "He is not the king. He will never be the king."

"Silence, you crazed old hag!" he yelled, his hand poised to strike her. Sidra stepped between them and, with every ounce of authority in her body, spoke.

"You will not strike her," she told him. "You will have your men untie her, and she will ride in the car with us."

"You are in no position to give orders, my love."

"I will give this order, and you will obey. Otherwise, you will need to kill us both right now. For I will never go with you willingly, should you kill Carlotta."

Piercing eyes searched hers, as if gauging her sincerity. At last, he motioned toward the trunk. "Untie the old woman. She will ride with us in the car," he told the driver, grasping Sidra's arm in a painful, viselike grip.

Once in the car, Carlotta kissed Sidra's hands and cheeks, overjoyed to see the woman she recognized as royalty instead of the child she had rescued so many years ago.

"Move back," Philippe said, nudging Carlotta's leg with his shoe. She winced but remained silent as she obeyed, moving away from Sidra with her head bowed in shame.

"Don't touch her again!" Sidra cried.

His shoe caught Sidra in the leg this time, and she gasped in pain.

"You seem to have forgotten who is in charge here, Princess," he told her. "We are playing by my rules now."

"When the little princess came, she was small and scared, covered with blood and tears. They followed her here, killed the others, and they meant to have the child as well."

"She's talking about me," Sidra breathed, leaning forward so she wouldn't miss a word of what Carlotta was saying.

"Yes, of course, she is," Philippe agreed.

"Who killed them, Carlotta?" Sidra prodded. "Who is after me?"

"They were horrible people, cruel and cold. They were determined they would have her. They killed my poor, sweet sister and left her body in the forest. They tried to find the child, but I had already found her and turned her into an American." Her thin pale lips turned up in a triumphant smile. "They would never recognize her as our princess."

"And yet they found her."

Carlotta's head snapped around at Philippe's observation, and her eyes blazed to life.

"Mateo!" She spat the word out as if it disgusted her, and Philippe's eyes grew even colder.

Just as suddenly as her moments of lucidity began, they ended, and Carlotta was lost once again. She turned her face away from them, seemingly fascinated by the scenery that flew by.

"What is Mateo?" Sidra asked him.

He shrugged nonchalantly.

"It is the name of an old and proud family in Medelia. Distant cousins of your mother's. Some say they should have ruled, but they were forced from power when the only girl child in their line was one born out of wedlock. Apparently, bastards can't be queen." He met her eyes, a dark warning within their depths. "Mateo is the name of the people who many suspected of your abduction. I believe Miriam and Gabriel discussed the theory with you."

"Yes, but I don't understand," she said. "Why would the Mateos have abducted me?"

"One of their young men, Jerald Mateo, was your fiancé. He died when he was only seventeen. Instead of honoring the bond between the families, your father betrothed you to another before Jerald was even buried."

"To you, you mean?"

He shook his head, and she gasped as she suddenly realized what he was saying.

179

"You are not Philippe Beauchene!"

"No. Philippe is still safe in Medelia, believing you are dead, and courting your cousin Estella. They have no idea you are alive after all these years and that, very shortly, you will be my bride."

"And if I refuse to marry you?"

"You, the old woman, and your lover will die."

****

Levi had never felt so helpless in his life. The ride to Jacksonville was the longest five hours of his life, and by the time they pulled into the airport terminal, he felt as if he'd run the entire way. His heart seemed to have ceased beating hours ago, and it now sat in a clenched, painful knot in his chest.

Miriam and Gabrielle had spent the first three hours detailing the cruelty of the Mateo family and how desperate Sidra's parents had been to keep her out of their clutches.

"By the time Jerald died, Jeanne and Rupert realized they could not let Sidra marry the next Mateo brother," Miriam explained. "Jerald's meanness and delusions had been blamed on his illness, but his younger brother, Vincente, had no such excuse. They say he has been cruel and filled with the lust for power since infancy. He will stop at nothing to gain the power he would have as king."

"But he is not her fiancé. How can he force her to marry him?"

"He will use the old woman. She will be his leverage and his tool to make Sidra do whatever it is he wants her to do."

Levi knew it was a cunningly effective tool.

"The Mateos are cousins who were once set to

inherit the crown. We share a common ancestor, a queen of Medelia who had two daughters. The younger was Jeanette, my great-grandmother. The older was the Mateos' great-grandmother. She had only one child, a son. His only child was an illegitimate daughter, born to a girl in their village. That child could never be queen, even though the Mateos believe she should have been. As it was, our great-grandmother had three female children, the youngest was my grandmother and the oldest was grandmother to Jeanne, Sidra's mother. The crown has been passed down to every oldest daughter for the last three generations and will go to the fourth when Sidra becomes queen."

Gabriel took up the explanation from there.

"While most of the Mateos have adjusted to my wife's branch of the family being the rulers, there has always been a small faction, all descendants of that one ill-bred daughter, who have felt disenfranchised and vengeful. They have threatened a coup for many years and, just before Sidra's birth, very nearly succeeded. It was then, in an attempt to broker peace, that Rupert and Jeanne bound the ties between Sidra and Jerald Mateo. At the time, he was nothing but a child, a boy of nine or ten, and his symptoms had not manifested themselves. Once they did, there was no choice to be had. If they wanted to maintain peace, Rupert and Jeanne had to let the betrothal proceed."

"How convenient that he killed himself," Levi said dryly.

Miriam looked startled, but she and Gabriel chose to ignore his words as Gabriel continued.

"Rupert hastily betrothed her to Philippe Beauchene, the young son of one of his most trusted advisors, but it became apparent within a few days that the Mateo faction was not going to accept it, so Rupert made a plan to get Sidra away from Medelia."

"He sent her here?" Levi could barely comprehend it. "She was a six-year-old child!"

"He didn't send her alone, Mr. Tanner. Her nanny accompanied her, and the two of them were to disappear until he sent for them to return to Medelia. I don't believe he ever thought the Mateos would follow her, or that she would be lost to us for twenty years. He believed that as time passed the faction would turn their attention to someone else."

"Like your daughter?"

"Yes, perhaps that is what Rupert hoped for, but it never happened. Soon after he and Jeanne received proof that Sidra had been killed, the Mateos faded into the background, and we have rarely heard of them since. The first and second generation of the faction died, and only Vincente is left."

"Who exactly is Vincente Mateo?"

"Vincente is Jerald's younger brother. He wants nothing so much as to be king, and he is perhaps crueler and more ruthless than Jerald."

"How much danger is Sidra in?" His heart froze as they both looked at him sadly.

"The moment she marries him, she's as good as dead."

"Why?" Levi demanded. "He can't gain the crown without her."

"We believe he has someone waiting to take her place, someone similar enough that Queen Marie, with her failing eyesight and high hopes, would never suspect the truth. After all, Sidra was only a child when she was taken from Medelia, and she has lived in America for many years. Vast changes are to be expected."

"But you've seen her. Surely he doesn't think you would keep quiet about it."

"Once he is king, it will no longer matter. Still, I am certain he has already arranged for our demise, as well," Gabriel informed him. "If we are lucky, our deaths will be quick and painless. I only pray we reach Medelia before it's done, as I would much prefer to die on my homeland's warm, golden shore."

"No one's going to die," Levi assured him. "Especially not Sidra."

They grew silent then, each one of them lost in their own thoughts as they sped toward Sidra and her captor.

He tried not to remember the photo of Sidra's nanny, tried not to imagine the torture and pain Vincente Mateo could be inflicting on Sidra at this very moment. Although he knew he was the gruffer half of Tanner and Tanner, he had never considered himself a violent man. Yet, as he thought of Sidra's smooth white flesh being torn and bruised, or pain riddling her body as she screamed in agony, he knew he could kill the man responsible.

For the first time in many months, he closed his eyes and prayed.

The airport came into view and Levi barked out orders for the driver to let him out at the gate. He refused to waste precious time parking and walking into the terminal. He had to find Sidra, and he meant to find her now.

He pushed his gun into Teddy's hands and leaped

from the car while it was still rolling.

He searched the sign for the next flight he thought they might be on, and chose the same one Miriam and Gabriel had planned to use. He dashed toward the gate, trying to move around it as the woman in charge commanded him to calm down.

It would only take him longer if they tackled him to the ground and carted him away, so he forced himself to stop and turn to her.

Panting from the run through the building, he tried to tell her he needed to speak with someone on the plane.

"No one has boarded yet, sir," she informed him. "The plane just arrived, and there is a forty-five-minute delay."

He was so relieved he nearly choked on the lump that formed in his throat.

"Thank you," he told her. "Thank you."

He looked around for a seat out of the way enough that he wouldn't be seen but could still have a view of the gate and every possible angle.

When he had decided on one, he went to it and dialed Teddy's cell phone.

"The plane hasn't boarded yet, so I'm going to wait here at the gate. They'll have to go through security, so I need you to stay nearby and let me know when you see them get in line. I don't want to alert Mateo to our presence until he's right here on me. I don't know what he'll do if he realizes we're onto him, and I don't want to risk him hurting Sidra or the old woman. Tell Miriam and Gabriel to move along the corridor between security and this gate. If they see them, I want them to keep their distance and call me immediately."

"You're no match to a gun, you know," Teddy warned.

"Yeah, I know. But there's not much chance he's getting a gun into the airport."

Chapter Twenty-One

Sidra walked beside Vincente, trying to remain as calm as possible with his mini-revolver resting against her side. She wasn't willing to find out how much damage the palm-sized gun could do to either her or Carlotta, so she did as he commanded and proceeded through the terminal, holding tightly to the old woman's hand.

Before leaving the car, he had forced her to dress herself and Carlotta in dark burkas, with veils that covered their faces. Their new attire exempted them from the security line. He had also removed his blond wig, transforming from a blond Adonis to an exotic, dark-haired prince.

Sidra's eyes darted about, searching for any escape route that might present itself. She nearly gasped in relief when her eyes caught sight of Teddy standing near the security line. His canes were nowhere in sight and he had an FSU ball cap pulled low over his face as he read a fishing magazine that blocked the view of his mouth. She stared hard at him, praying he would look up, fighting the urge to scream when he straightened from the wall as if he'd seen her but then looked past her to a blond woman walking toward them.

Disappointment colored his face when he realized the woman wasn't her, and he relaxed and lifted the magazine once more. Praying her ruse would catch his attention without sending a bullet through either her or Carlotta, she tripped forward, catching herself just before she hit the ground. Since she was holding Carlotta's hand, the poor old woman lurched forward too, and a cry of dismay escaped her lips as Sidra twisted to catch her.

Over Carlotta's shoulder, her eyes met Teddy's, but before she could tell if he recognized her or not, Vincente jerked both of them to their feet and was once again forcing them down the hall.

As they passed an empty waiting area, he jerked her behind a small wall divider that hid them from view of the passing crowd. He backhanded her, hard, across her cheek with his empty hand, then raised it to Carlotta.

Ignoring the pain that shot through her cheekbone and the warm trickle of blood, she met his cold green eyes.

"You touch her, and I'll raise such a ruckus you'll have to kill us both right here in the airport," she promised him. "I know you'll kill me eventually, but you will have little chance of escaping alive if you do it here."

He lowered his hand and stepped back as triumph trumpeted through her. They were safe for now.

Just before they reached the gate, he stopped and turned away, leading them in the opposite direction.

"Where are we going?" she demanded. If Teddy was here, Levi was here. And the logical place for Levi to await them was at the gate where they would board.

"I've changed my mind about flying to Paris," he said. "Rome will work just as well, and we won't run as much risk of someone following us."

"Rome, Rome, Rome," Carlotta began to mumble. She peered at him through her veil. "I knew a man from Rome. He had eyes like yours. Do you know him, boy? Do you know my Antone?"

"Shut up!" he hissed, but she kept rambling on.

"He was a man among men," she crowed. "A man any woman would throw herself at. He had so many women. I was only one of them."

"If you don't shut her up, I'll kill her."

"Carlotta, hush," she soothed. "You can tell me about Antone later."

"You know him, then?" The rheumy eyes brightened.

"Yes, of course."

"Ah-ha!" she laughed, a wicked gleam in her eyes. "You have known him, too."

She spoke his name quickly and repeatedly under her breath as they walked, and several people looked their way as they passed.

"He gave me a child," Carlotta confided. "A boy child with hair as black as night and eyes—"

"Shut her up," Vincente hissed again, sounding panicked as the pistol moved up her side.

He was becoming nervous, and Sidra was suddenly reminded of something she'd learned long ago. Dangerous people were even more dangerous when they felt cornered or nervous for some reason. She had watched children come into the homes where she lived, and many times if they were prone to lash out, it happened when they felt they were losing control.

"It's okay," she soothed. "She's an old woman. People will realize she has dementia. They won't pay her any attention."

"Is the lady all right, sir?" a familiar masculine voice said from behind them, and Sidra nearly collapsed under the crushing wave of relief that swamped her.

"Of course," Vincente turned to Levi with a patronizing smile. "You must excuse my mother-in-law. She has lost much of her mind and repeats her dead lover's name day and night."

"Sorry to bother you, then. I just wanted to make sure you didn't need any help."

"Thank you for your concern, but I assure you we would ask for assistance if it were needed."

She fought back tears of frustration and fear as she realized Levi was walking away. He hadn't recognized Vincente as Philippe, and there was no way he could have recognized her. He had been a hair's breadth away, and she had allowed him to walk away. But the fear that Vincente would kill him along with her and Carlotta had forced her to remain silent.

"Sidra!" Levi's voice echoed around them, and her breath caught in her throat. "Sidra!"

She swung around, her eyes meeting his across the busy terminal. He stalked toward her, eyes blazing with determination as Vincente lifted the gun away from her side. The barrel caught a ray of light, and someone near them screamed.

"Gun!"

The gun made hardly a sound when he pulled the trigger.

"No!" she screeched as Carlotta crumpled to the ground beside her. "No!"

Screaming and footsteps filled her mind as Vincente threw her across his shoulder and ran. He would never escape, and she guessed he knew it as well as she did, but he ran anyway, determined to try. His shoulder pounded against her chest and stomach, knocking the air out of her with each impact, making her dizzy and ill.

"Mateo!" Levi yelled from just behind them, and somehow Vincente managed to twist around and fire a shot toward him.

She heard Levi's grunt and low curse as the bullet caught him, but his footsteps barely slowed as Vincente burst through a doorway onto the tarmac.

They were in the open now, police officers surrounding them from every direction. She was as bound to die as he was in a hailstorm of bullets and gunfire.

The first shot caught him in the knee, and he stumbled but righted himself. His breath was coming in hard, deep pants, and she wondered why he didn't throw her down. It couldn't be easy to run with her over his shoulder, yet he kept a death grip on her as he ran toward a small plane nearby.

The second bullet pierced his back, and he dropped to his knees, a groan of pain issuing from somewhere deep inside. Still he held her, and although she fought against his grip, he held her tight. Then Levi was nearly on them, rushing toward them, and she felt Vincente shift, his arm lifted, and she screamed out a warning as he turned.

"Levi! No!"

The bullet that hit Vincente's temple sent him toppling forward, bringing Sidra to the ground with him as he fell.

Her head hit the pavement, and she saw stars as she

heard running footsteps and frantic voices racing toward her.

"Sidra!" Levi was beside her, his hands rolling Vincente's body away from her and helping her to her feet.

"You're hurt," she cried when she saw the blood that stained the side of his shirt.

"It's nothing," he assured her, but, in contrast to his words, his face was pale and drawn with pain.

She wrapped her arms around him, holding him against her as the police surrounded them.

Chapter Twenty-Two

It was nearly dawn when Sidra and Teddy walked toward the airport entrance. Gabriel and Miriam were in a rental car, headed to a hotel, and would be leaving for Medelia on the flight they already had scheduled.

Sidra had promised them she would follow on a later flight. She hadn't told them how much later, because she had no idea if it would be hours, days, or weeks. Right now, she just needed to get to Levi, who had been taken to the hospital while the rest of them were confined in a small room off the airport's main terminal.

It had taken hours for their identities to be confirmed, with many phone calls between the officers who questioned them and Medelian officials. At last, the questioning ended, arrangements were made for Carlotta's body, and they were all released.

Sidra had traded the burka and veil for a flowered elastic-thread dress and a pair of rubber flip-flops she'd purchased from the airport gift shop. Miriam had offered her the bag of makeup from her purse when she'd asked for a hairbrush, but Sidra had refused it. Why waste good makeup when her hair was limp and in desperate need of shampoo, her face was bruised, and a large, angry cut marred one cheek? She was going straight to the hospital to see Levi, and once she was certain he was okay, she would go to a hotel, where she hoped for a nice hot bath and a good night's sleep. The bath was a given, but the sleep wasn't. Even now, if she closed her eyes, she heard the gunfire, felt Carlotta's body fall away from her to the floor, and saw Levi coming toward her pale and bleeding. Although the officers had assured her Levi was fine, she needed to see him herself.

She breathed a sigh of relief as the doors slid open, but within seconds she was engulfed in the chaos of glaring lights and microphones as reporters swarmed them.

"Is it true you're the long-lost princess of Medelia?" a woman called.

"What can you tell us about the man who died here today?"

"Have you spoken to your family since you were found?"

Rendered mute by surprise, Sidra stopped and stared at them.

"Come on, Sid," Teddy urged, guiding her forward with a hand at her waist.

"Sir, are you one of the men who rescued her? How did it happen?"

"We have no comment at the moment," Teddy told them, and with an authority that belied his limping swagger, he pushed through the crowd to the parking garage.

"Good grief," she muttered when they pulled out of the darkened interior and were greeted by more flashing cameras and reporters. "They're like a swarm of bees."

"You can't blame them, can you? How often does a long-lost princess surface?" He grinned at her. "Not that anyone would guess you were a princess right now."

She chuckled as she looked down at her exposed knees. She could almost hear Carlotta's voice telling her how a lady should dress.

"When you stand, your knees should be covered, Sidra," Carlotta had told her many years ago. She had demonstrated with her own dark polyester skirt. "Sitting will naturally raise the hem, and you must never expose more than the proper amount of flesh."

The lessons had continued as Carlotta taught her the necessity of hose and the proper way to cross her legs.

"Are you okay, Sid?"

"Not really," she admitted. "But I'm sure I will be. I just can't believe Carlotta's dead. She taught me so much. It never occurred to me that she could be more than just a caseworker. Looking back, I guess I should have realized it."

"Levi told us on our drive down how special she was to you. It seems like she worked hard to keep both your identities a secret."

"I never questioned how she found me," she said now. "I wonder if she would have told me if I had. Her sister died trying to protect me, yet she was willing to take me on anyway. Do you think she minded carrying the secret of my identity alone all these years?"

"If she hadn't cared, or if she had wanted to be rid of you, she could have just put you somewhere and left you. Instead, she moved you each year, or whenever she felt it necessary, to make sure no one got close enough to find out your secret. She put herself at risk every day she remained in your life."

The tears Sidra had been battling spilled over her

cheeks, and she nodded her head in agreement. "I just wish she hadn't died that way. She deserved a more dignified, painless passing. But because of me, her death was violent and frightening."

"It wasn't your fault, Sidra."

She tried to tell herself he was right, maybe it wasn't, but that didn't change the fact that Carlotta had died because of her.

They rode the last few blocks in silence, and when they pulled to a stop in the hospital parking lot, Sidra practically ran to the elevator, pushing the button and holding the doors open while Teddy caught up. The closer she got to Levi, the faster her heart beat, until she came to the door of his room, where she stopped to catch her breath.

Teddy was coming down the hall at a slower pace, a smile on his handsome face.

"Don't let me stop you," he said with a chuckle. "Go ahead in."

She didn't hesitate for another minute. With a soft rap on the door, she entered, nearly running into a middle-aged nurse coming out of the room with a small tray caring a hypodermic needle and a glass vial.

"I hope you're Sidra," the woman said. "If you're not, don't expect a warm welcome."

"I am," she said, soliciting a soft cluck of sympathy and a pat on the back.

"You've got your hands full with that one," the nurse said. "But he has just been shot, and you don't look much better than he does, so maybe he's worth the hassle on a good day."

"Maybe," Sidra answered with a grin. If he was well enough to give the nurse a hard time, he was going to be fine.

The nurse closed the door behind her, leaving Sidra standing beside it. Levi was sitting up in bed wearing a pale blue hospital gown, an intravenous drip in his arm and a monitor flashing his vitals behind him. He looked a bit pale but quite healthy for a man who had just been shot. He also looked mad as hell.

"Get over here," he ordered, and she obeyed without a thought.

When she was close enough, his hand reached to catch her around the waist and pull her to him.

"I thought you'd never get here," he said as he caught her mouth with his. He kissed her hungrily, as if he couldn't get enough of her lips.

"Me either. I was about to go crazy before they finally let us go." She cupped his face in her hands, trying to look angry but knowing she failed miserably. How could she possibly frown when he was here, alive and looking as good as ever? "Oh, Levi, you could have been killed."

"Not with that little peashooter he was carrying." He kissed each of her wrists. His eyes searched her face, darkening noticeably when they fell on the cuts and bruises Vincente had left there. "I wish they hadn't killed the bastard. I'd have liked a few minutes alone with him myself."

"No, don't even think it. He wasn't the kind of man who would fight fair. He would have killed you without batting an eye."

She tried to come to terms with the fact that she was glad a man was dead. Did that make her a horrible person?

"Good to see you looking so happy to be alive,

bro," Teddy joked from the doorway. "How long are you in for?"

"I can leave tomorrow, barring any complications. They removed the bullet, and I'm getting antibiotics right now." He lifted the arm with the I.V. "The bullet didn't do much damage, but the doctor was worried it could get infected. He decided we should err on the side of caution."

"Well, with that kind of good news, it seems like you could be a little happier."

"Go to hell, Ted," Levi shot back. "I'm happy."

Teddy laughed and sat in the chair near the window.

"What the hell do you think he was he thinking, using a miniature gun like that in a kidnapping?" Teddy asked casually, although Levi sensed a bigger question behind his words.

"He was thinking he only had to use it to get two women to do what he told them. He relied on the threat more than how he'd carry it out."

"He killed Carlotta, and you're in the hospital," Sidra reminded them. "So it wasn't completely harmless."

"I'm sorry about Carlotta, sweetheart," Levi said softly.

"Me too." She sat on the edge of the bed and took his hand. "But I'm so glad you're okay."

Tears sprang to her eyes, and she bent her head, studying his hands in hers, following the lines of his fingers and veins. The gentle stroke of her fingers across his hand sent tiny whirls of electricity through his body.

"Are your cousins leaving for Medelia as

planned?" He tried not to sound as affected by her touch as he felt.

"Yes." She lifted her forlorn face to his, and his heart tightened with dread. This was it. She was about to tell him she was leaving.

"And you?"

"No. Not yet. I have things I need to do for Carlotta, and I want to make sure my house is taken care of before I leave."

"So what are we looking at? A few weeks?" he asked hopefully.

"More like a few days. My neighbor will look after the house, and the funeral should be over by the end of the week."

"So we have what? Six days?"

She shook her head. "I don't know. Maybe I should wait a while, take some classes or something."

"What kind of classes?"

"The kind a princess needs." She looked positively terrified. "I have no idea how to be a princess. My grandmother may be horrified."

He turned his hand up and caught hers in it. "Your grandmother will be too overjoyed to see you to be worried about how princess-like you are or aren't."

He prayed that was true. He still couldn't imagine her father willingly sending her away. Even if he hadn't expected her to be gone twenty years, it certainly wasn't as if he expected her to be gone only a few days. He had to have known she would be gone for months, possibly even years. How had he decided that was a good plan? And had he or his wife ever once considered giving up their claim on the throne so that her arranged marriage could be forfeited?

His mind raced with questions, but his heart filled with dread. She had to know her father sent her here, and it would be better if he told her now so she had time to get used to the idea before returning to Medelia.

"Sidra," he began, but something in his voice must have frightened her, because she shook her head vehemently.

"No more tonight."

His willpower was no match for the earnest plea in her voice.

"No more for tonight," he murmured in agreement, brushing her hair out of her face. "Go to the hotel and get a good night's sleep. We'll talk about it all in the morning."

"That is the best idea I've heard all day," Teddy agreed with false joviality. His eyes met Levi's over Sidra's shoulder in an unspoken message of solidarity.

They might still have their differences, but they were together on this. Sidra was their number-one priority, and neither of them was convinced she was completely out of danger. He would have to trust Teddy to keep her safe for tonight, but tomorrow he'd be back at her side, and he'd be damned if she was going anywhere alone, including Medelia.

****

Sidra flipped on the hotel television as she went toward the bathroom. She and Teddy had stopped at a small variety store on the way to the hotel to purchase overnight necessities, and the smell of the rose-chamomile bubble bath scented the air of her room. She could hardly wait to soak in the tub and let the warm, aromatic water ease the ache from her body and soul.

She gave a sigh of relief as she sank into the water.

She hurt from head to toe, but she was alive, and for that she was grateful. Although both Levi and Teddy had assured her he wasn't ever in danger from dying, she didn't believe for a minute that he couldn't have been more seriously injured, and just the thought of him dying for her was more than she could bear.

She closed her eyes and replayed the day, everything she'd learned, and the things she still didn't understand. For a few moments following Vincente's death, she'd believed the questions were answered. But as the shock wore off and the hours passed, she realized she had more questions than ever.

Her questions all centered on the things Carlotta had said. Things she wasn't even sure were true. Had a man told her to watch for Sidra and to keep her safe? If so, who in the world could he have been? Were the Mateos the reason she had moved from one home to the next so often? Had they really tried to find her all those years?

If they had known where to look, why on earth hadn't her parents been able to find her? To be fair, Gabriel and Miriam had found her four years ago, but why had it taken them so long?

She tried to remember anything new about her childhood. Anything besides a cruel ride on a carousel, a man's body, and Nanny's murder, but she hit a wall, and even those memories seemed fuzzy and unreachable.

Exhaustion weighted her limbs and made her head fuzzy as she climbed out of the tub, slipped on a nightgown, and staggered toward the bed. Through the cotton in her head, she heard a familiar voice, and she turned to stare at the television, where Gabriel was standing in front of the airport, talking to a news crew in an uncharacteristically emotional voice.

Her eyes fell to the newsfeed at the bottom of the screen, and she felt as if the floor had dropped out from under her.

Gabriel De Leone, Husband of Woman Killed.

She sank onto the end of the bed as a reporter recapped the story of her cousin's murder.

"As you heard, Mr. De Leone and his wife were robbed and Mrs. De Leone was killed this morning outside their hotel room. Ironically, their cousin, Princess Sidra of Medelia, was involved in a fatal shootout here at the Jacksonville International Airport last night. The two incidents are not thought to be related. The suspects were last seen traveling north on I-95 in a silver pickup truck. Miriam Carbone De Leone was shot and killed when she refused to give the robbers her jewelry. The suspects are described as white men in their early thirties, with tattoos on their arms and necks. Please notify the police if you see anyone matching the suspects' description."

Chapter Twenty-Three

Levi flipped the television off, praying Sidra was asleep and not watching the news. If she didn't know already, she would soon enough, and he needed to be with her either way. He hit the call button again, and the nurse's irritated voice came over the speaker.

"Mr. Tanner, the doctor has signed the discharge papers, and your nurse will be down as soon as possible to remove your IV line. Please have a little patience."

He grabbed the phone and punched in Teddy's cell phone number.

"Damn it, Teddy, answer the phone." He slammed it back down and hit the call button again.

"Mr. Tanner—" The nurse's voice held a heated warning, but Levi interrupted her.

"I need the name of the nearest hotel."

She sighed heavily but gave him one that was only a couple of blocks away, on the river.

"Do you have the phone number?"

Dead, angry silence filled his ear.

"Give it to me, and I promise I'll quit calling you."

"Fine. I'm looking it up."

After he had the number, he called the hotel and asked to be connected to Teddy's room. The phone rang five times before Teddy finally picked up.

"Hello?" His voice was groggy from sleep, but Levi paid little heed to that.

"Where's Sidra?"

"In the room next door. I made her leave the door between us cracked so I could hear her if she needed me." His voice sharpened. "God almighty, Levi, you aren't back to suspecting her and me of being lovers, are you?"

"No. Have you watched the news?"

"I haven't watched anything. I think I was asleep before we got here. Getting into bed was just a formality."

"Miriam was killed this morning."

"What?"

"I just saw it on the news. Gabriel claims they were robbed outside their hotel room near the airport, and Miriam was shot during the robbery. But that's a bit too much coincidence for me to believe."

"What do you need me to do?"

"I need you to go to Sidra's room and make sure she's okay. Call me back here." He breathed a sigh of relief as the nurse came through the doors.

The phone rang as the nurse was reciting instructions on how to care for his wound, and she glared at him when he answered it with a curt hello.

"She's here, fast asleep."

He hadn't realized he was holding his breath until he heard his brother's assurance that Sidra was safe.

"Thank God," he breathed. "I'll be there as soon as I can."

"I'll stay here in case she wakes up."

"Yeah, yeah, that'll be great."

He looked at the nurse as he hung up the phone.

"Can I continue now?" she asked him, her narrow eyebrows disappearing under her brows.

"No," he said. "Just get this damn thing out of my arm."

"I have to read this."

"No, you don't. I can read it when I leave. Right now, I've got to get out of here."

When she opened her mouth to protest, he took a deep breath and yanked the IV from his arm.

With an outraged screech, she grabbed some gauze and a bandage and covered the tiny bruised hole. She stuffed the discharge papers into his hands and stalked toward the door.

"Good-bye, Mr. Tanner. And good luck."

He didn't have time to worry about whether he'd hurt the nurse's feelings. Something didn't feel right about Miriam's death, Sidra needed him, and all he could think about was getting to her. He dressed quickly, deciding against wearing the bloodstained shirt, which he threw into the garbage can, and hurried outside.

The river was easy enough to see from the hospital, and he moved toward it, ending up on a concrete walk that ran beside it. He asked a passing jogger for directions to the hotel and then walked as fast as he could toward it, ignoring the mixture of curious and appreciative glances he received from the people walking along the path.

He called Teddy's cell phone on his way through the lobby, then took the elevator to the floor Teddy told him. The room was at the end of the hall, and he jogged toward it, cringing at the small jolts of pain the movement caused.

Teddy opened the door before he knocked. He gripped Levi's hand firmly in greeting and gave him a pat on the back.

"I'll be in my room," he said before slipping out the door, leaving Levi alone with Sidra.

He took a step closer and looked down at her while she slept. Her face wasn't as badly bruised as it had appeared last night, but her eyes were puffy and red-rimmed, with dark shadows beneath them. Tear stains tracked her cheeks, and he wished he had been there to hold her as she cried. He hated to wake her, hated to start her day with the news he had to share. Maybe it would be better just to let her sleep for a while. He removed his pants and climbed into bed beside her, smiling as she turned toward him. He placed a soft kiss on her forehead, and she sighed contentedly as she snuggled to him.

"Don't let me hurt you," she mumbled against his chest.

"You won't."

She grew silent and still once more, and he hoped she had fallen back to sleep.

"Did you see the news?" she asked quietly.

"Yes."

"I think he killed her."

He was surprised by her quiet confession. He had expected her to balk at the suggestion.

"Why do you think that?"

"I don't know. I just don't trust him."

"Yeah, me neither."

"I don't want to leave this bed."

"We don't have to yet. We both need sleep so we can think with a clear head."

"I don't want to sleep, either."

He chuckled and rubbed his cheek against the top

of her hair, inhaling the sweet feminine scent of her shampoo.

"Sorry, sweetheart, but they doped me up on enough painkillers last night that I don't think anything else is going to happen right now."

"Mmmm." She kissed his chest. "I'm not getting out of this bed until it does."

"Deal," he murmured, sleep already claiming him.

****

Sidra came awake slowly, luxuriating in the feel of Levi's warm, hard body next to her. She ran a foot down his leg, letting it move across the top of his toes before bringing it back upward.

He turned and wrapped an arm around her waist, his face in her hair. She felt his mouth turn up into a teasing smile.

"Again?" His voice was low and sexy against her ear, and she shivered with desire when his breath tickled her skin.

At some point in the afternoon, they had made slow, easy love to each other, giving and taking, asking and receiving, until they had fallen back asleep, satisfied, content, and more than a little dazed.

"I'm starving." She flopped to her stomach and propped her chin on her hands.

"For me?" He wiggled his eyebrows suggestively.

"For food," she said with a grin. "And you. Food first, though, or I might just keel over from hunger right in the middle of it."

"Mmm, we can't have that," he said, lifting up on his elbow and kissing her shoulder and back. "You smell good."

"Not as good as a steak would smell right now."

He chuckled and sat up on the edge of the bed. "Fine, I'll feed you before I do anything else to you."

"Good idea." She jumped out of bed and pulled the gown over her head.

"Sidra," he called softly. "You know we're going to have to talk about Miriam eventually."

She swallowed back the denial. Of course they would have to face it, but she couldn't right now. She was afraid of what it all meant, and for just a little while longer she needed to pretend it meant nothing.

"I know, but I can't right now." She bit her lip, holding it for a moment before adding, "I just need a little while longer to pretend things can be normal, Levi. Then we'll talk."

Worry furrowed his brow, but he nodded, and she breathed a sigh of relief.

"I'll give you 'til tomorrow morning, Sid. Then it's back to reality."

****

As soon as she was in the shower, he dialed Teddy's room.

"Hey, Ted, are you up for supper? We're going to head downstairs to the restaurant when we're dressed."

"Is Sidra okay?"

"She seems fine, but she doesn't want to talk about it. I promised her a reprieve until morning."

"It's been a hell of a few days," Teddy agreed. "I think we could all use a few more hours to recover."

"We'll meet you downstairs."

Teddy was silent for a long minute before he cleared his throat. "Levi, what are you planning on doing here? I mean, Sidra's different from the girls you usually see."

"Is this the 'what are your intentions toward my daughter' talk?" Levi chuckled in disbelief. Could his younger brother really be about to lecture him on treating Sidra right? "This coming from the guy who reeled her in and lied to her for the last four years."

"That's not the same, and you know it. I was protecting her. You could easily destroy her."

He could hear the worry in Teddy's voice, and he grew serious himself.

"I'm not going to hurt her, Ted. If she'll have me, I intend to marry her."

Teddy breathed a loud sigh of relief.

"Thank God. I'd hate to have to kick your ass."

"I'd hate to see you try."

"Yeah, whatever. See ya."

Levi hung up the phone and sauntered to the bathroom. Sidra stuck her head out from behind the shower curtain, her gaze running appreciatively over his naked body. When she reached his eyes, she smiled and crooked a finger in his direction.

"Call Teddy back and tell him we'll be late," she said as he joined her.

"No way," he teased as he nuzzled her neck. "I can't have you passing out from hunger."

"Then you'd better work fast." She giggled as he yanked her up against him and did exactly what she suggested.

****

"Could we have a table across the room?" Levi asked the waitress as she led them toward a booth beside the glowing Christmas tree.

"Of course, sir," she said, a puzzled look on her smiling face.

"No," Sidra said. "Let's sit near the tree."

"Are you sure?" Levi asked.

"Yes, I'm sure I'll be fine."

She walked confidently toward the table, even taking a moment to study the tree before having a seat.

"You did great," he said after the waitress left with their drink order.

"Maybe finding a reason for my recurrent fears during the holidays helped ease them."

They made small talk while they waited for their food, discussing things that were as far removed as possible from Medelia and all that had happened in the last few days.

Levi watched Sidra's face, noting the worry that crept in during lulls in the conversation, and the way her eyes darted to the door now and then. She wasn't any more convinced she was out of danger than he and Teddy were. He wanted to ask her why, but he had promised her tonight, and he would give it to her.

"Do you think we should go to Gabriel?" she asked. "I mean, he is alone here, and if he didn't kill Miriam, someone did, and he must be in horrible pain."

"We aren't going anywhere tonight," he told her. "But if it will make you feel better, Teddy can call and check on him after we eat."

Teddy's cell phone rang just as they were leaving the restaurant.

"Yes, I know him. Yes, we'll be there in a few minutes." Before he hung up, he added, "Hey, man, can you make sure he stays right there? Thanks."

"Who was it?"

"It was the bartender at a bar out by the airport. Seems old Gabe's had a few too many, and he's causing quite a ruckus. My number was the only number from Florida in his phone, so they called me."

****

"Spill, Sid. What's got you so antsy tonight?"

Sidra knew with one glance there was no use denying it.

"I thought I had a reprieve."

"Yeah, well, Gabriel ruined that for you."

"I'm nervous it isn't over yet. I know Vincente's dead, and I know he tried to kidnap me, but he didn't intend to kill me. Well, at least not until after we were married. So who did intend to?"

"I have the same feeling," Levi admitted. "I mean, the guy at the bus stop hasn't been seen yet. He could have been working for Vincente, but he could have just as easily been working for someone else. The car that tried to run you down and the guys shooting at you were all trying to do more than scare or abduct you."

"So you don't think I'm out of danger?"

"No," Levi and Teddy answered at the same time.

They turned onto the road to the airport, surprised to find a traffic jam at this time of night.

"There must be an accident," Levi said. "I can see flashing lights up ahead."

They crept along, braking every few feet. Each stop caused Sidra's anxiety to grow. Something horrible had happened. Finally, when they were nearly there, Teddy's phone rang again.

"Shit," he moaned into the phone. "Yeah, thanks for letting us know."

"It's Gabriel, isn't it?" Sidra asked, but she knew. Whoever had killed Miriam had come back for him.

"Yeah. Sid, I'm sorry. He's dead. The bartender

said he left his cell phone on the counter and wandered outside. The man went out to try to catch him, but it was too late. A passing car hit Gabriel as he left the parking lot. The car didn't stop, but the witnesses say it was a long, black sedan."

"Damn it!" Levi pulled into the turning lane and did a u-turn in the opposite direction.

"Where are you going?" Sidra cried.

"We're going to Gulfview, where I know how to hide you and who's friend and foe."

Chapter Twenty-Four

"Home sweet home," Levi announced as they turned onto his parents' street.

Sidra looked longingly at the Lawrence house as they passed it. Had it really been only three nights ago that she and Levi had stood just outside it as he asked her if she would consider living there with him? So much had happened in that time. The whole week had been a whirlwind, and she felt as if she had been tossed about and beaten by the storm.

She turned her attention to Levi's profile, and her heart swelled with love. She would never be able to live without him, but she had no idea what the next few days or even months held.

They drove up to the Tanner house, and Levi groaned when the broken window and charred wood of the breakfast nook came into sight. Just as she saw the red sports car in the carport to the side of the house, another groan escaped him.

"Mom and Dad are back."

He'd no sooner said it than his mom flew out the front door, barely waiting for him to come to a stop before she was pulling Teddy's door open.

"Oh, thank God, you're all okay!" she cried, throwing her arms around Teddy and then Sidra, who was climbing out of the back seat. Finally, she hurried around the back of the car and threw her arms around

Levi. She hugged him as if she might never let him go, before promptly bursting into tears.

"Mom, it's all right. We're all fine. I'm sorry about the house."

"The house? I don't give a fig about the house. I was so worried about you and Teddy, and, oh, Sidra, I'm so glad you're fine. We saw everything on the news last night—the shootout at the airport, and that poor woman being killed, and now they're saying her husband was killed too. We came right home, but when I saw the kitchen, I was so frightened something horrible had happened."

"Which I told her didn't make any sense when we had just seen Teddy and Sidra on television last night," her husband chimed in.

"But they said someone had been shot and taken to the hospital." She took a shuddering breath. "I just can't go through having one of my children being hurt like that again."

"I was shot, Mom, but it's no big deal," Levi assured her. "It was a small, clean wound, and I'm just a little sore today. It hasn't slowed me down at all."

"I'm so sorry I caused you so much worry, Mrs. Tanner," Sidra said, moving to stand beside Levi.

His mom hugged her again. "Is what the news said true? Were you really kidnapped as a child? Are you really a princess?"

"Yes, but I barely remember any of it. Even my parents." Her voice broke, and with a murmur of sympathy, Betty Tanner pulled her back into a warm embrace.

****

"Do you think you'll be home for Christmas?"

Betty asked as Sidra helped her put the finishing touches on supper.

"I'm not even sure I know where home is anymore," Sidra answered candidly.

Betty tilted her head to look at her, a knowing smile on her face.

"I think you know exactly where home is." She chuckled. "If you're not here with him for Christmas, I hope to see you by the New Year."

Sidra blushed. "Am I that obvious?"

"Not just you. He's got it bad himself. I can't remember him ever being so crazy about someone." She lowered her voice. "You know, he's planning to put a bid in on the Lawrence place. Claims it's perfect for a princess. Teddy will tease him unmercifully for that."

"But he's right," Sidra said. "It is the stuff fairy tales and little girls' dreams are made of. It is perfectly perfect."

"And close by, so my next batch of grandchildren can be properly spoiled."

Warmth rushed up Sidra's neck and burned in her face.

"Do you really think that's what he wants?"

"Yes. But first he wants you safe and settled. So go to Medelia and sort this mess out. When I think about what your poor mother suffered all those years, I feel so sorry for her. To think you were abducted and killed! I can't even imagine how horrible that must have been."

"I grew up thinking I was abandoned by my parents. It's never been easy for me to believe anyone loved or wanted me." She sighed. "Until Teddy found me. He and Levi didn't just hire me, they took me in and made me part of their little world. They accepted me and loved me. And both of them risked their lives for me."

"That's what families do." She patted Sidra's back as she passed her on the way to the refrigerator. "I think you just might have saved Levi's life, too. Thank you for being there for him the last few months. I've been so worried about him, but knowing you were there made it easier."

"I wouldn't have left him."

Teddy came through the door, his eyes shooting between them.

"Is this one of those chick-flick moments? Where all the women in the audience are crying and all the men are wondering what the hell's going on?"

"No, you goof, this is the moment when you tell your dad dinner is ready," Betty said, and Sidra burst out laughing.

Chapter Twenty-Five

Dawn had barely lightened the sky when Sidra opened her eyes. A cold front had swooped in overnight, and she shivered as she snuggled closer to Levi's body. He lay on his side, facing her, and she laid a hand on his face, letting it move slowly down his neck and over the contours of his chest and arms.

His low hum of pleasure was followed by a soft snore, and she smiled to herself before slipping from the bed and tiptoeing down the hall to the playroom. She had gone to sleep there, but Levi had retrieved her later, carrying her down the hall and depositing her in his bed, as if he were the hero in one of the romance novels she loved so much. Although his parents seemed like realistic people, she didn't feel comfortable with them finding her in bed with their son, and she prayed no one witnessed her guilty retreat.

Longing for some cool, fresh air, she pulled on a pair of jeans, a sweatshirt, and sneakers. She scribbled a hasty note telling Levi she had gone for a walk and placed it on the kitchen counter where he would see it. Then she let herself out of the house and headed down the road toward town.

The only thing open at this hour was a convenience store and a small café next door. Before she could talk herself out of it, she marched into the café and sat at the counter.

"What's it going to be, sweetie?" the short, plump waitress asked.

"Coffee, please, no sugar, and just a touch of cream. And a jelly donut."

"Aren't you Levi Tanner's girl?" asked the woman—Val according to her laminated nametag.

"Yes." The answer felt so good she laughed out loud. She was Levi's girl. "I'm Sidra Martin."

"I saw you on the news. Is it true you're a princess?"

"I think so, yes."

"So who were the man and woman who came to town looking for you? Some relation? They were as hoity-toity as they come."

"Yes, Miriam and I were cousins."

"What about the other guy? He had dinner with them just the other night. When was it? Oh, I know, it was the night of the home tours. I remember him saying something about Sidra going on the tour when I was taking an order from the table next to them." She smiled sheepishly. "You can't help but listen when people like that come in. It just seems like they lead such exciting lives, you hate to miss anything. And with that accent, who could resist hanging on his every word?"

Sidra was thankful when the doorbell tinkled and a large group of construction workers piled inside the café. While she drank her coffee and ate her donut, she tried to think about what it meant that Miriam and Gabriel had eaten dinner with Vincente Mateo. After a few minutes, she knew she wouldn't reach any conclusions amidst the growing din of customers in the café. She stood to go, but before she did, she motioned for Val. She had to confirm one thing that niggled at the back of her mind.

"I was just wondering what the man looked like, the one my cousins had dinner with."

Expecting to hear something about a good-looking man with green eyes, she was shocked at Val's description.

"He was a big guy, though not real tall, with big, meaty hands and dark hair."

Though she knew the answer, she had to ask anyway. "What color were his eyes?"

"They were dark, hon, nearly black."

"Thank you." Her throat dry with fear, she rushed from the café, hoping to flee the knowledge that Miriam and Gabriel had eaten dinner with the man who had tried to kill her.

She was a block away from the café when she realized she was being tailed by a vehicle.

She ducked into a small five-and-dime that had just opened for the day, and walked around hoping they'd leave. The shopkeeper watched her closely, as if he were afraid she might stuff something in her pocket at any moment, while her eyes darted to the window every few minutes.

"Can I help you, miss?" he called from behind the counter.

"No, thank you. I'm just looking."

He narrowed his eyes at her but said nothing more as she grabbed a basket and began placing things inside.

Finally, the car pulled away, and she went to the counter.

"May I use your telephone?"

"Don't you got a cell?" the old man grumbled.

"No, sir."

"Fine, but it better be local."

She smiled and dialed Levi's phone, speaking quickly when he picked up, his voice furious.

"Where the hell are you?"

"Levi, listen to me. I'm at the five-and-dime store in town, and I need you to come get me. The waitress said Gabriel and Miriam had dinner with a big dark-haired man. Do you think it was the man who tried to kidnap me? Now there's someone following me, and I'm scared to death to go outside. But why would he still be after me? Vincente's dead."

"Damn it, Sidra, you are going to get yourself killed!"

"Are you coming or not?"

"I'll be there in five minutes. Do not leave that store until I get there."

He had nothing to worry about. She wouldn't leave the relative safety of the store for all the money in the world.

****

Levi had never been so angry in his life. Sidra should know better than to leave without telling anyone where she was going. Hadn't she learned anything from the last few days? The man who'd tried to abduct her from the bus station was still out there, still trying to finish the job he'd most likely been hired to do. She should have known she wouldn't be safe until that man was found or until they at least knew who had paid him. Although if he had eaten dinner with Miriam and Gabriel, there wasn't much question about who was footing his bill. How could Sidra have been so foolish as to traipse to town on her own?

He tried to tell himself she was used to living alone and even to working alone, for the most part. She was independent and had taken care of herself for years now, but nothing he said to himself calmed him. It only made him more furious.

If he were to be honest with himself, he knew he would realize his fury had more to do with the fact that she was already pulling away from him than with her disregard for her safety. After all, they had thought perhaps the danger was gone now that Vincente, Miriam, and Gabriel were all dead.

He had been disappointed when he woke up to an empty bed, but he had expected her to be downstairs. When he found the note instead of her, it had been like a caution light, warning him the end of the road was near.

Maybe Teddy was right when he said he was overreacting, but he couldn't make himself believe it. To him, it felt like the first step on his way back to being alone. He hadn't noticed it happening the first time around, when he had just turned around one day and everyone was gone—Teddy, his parents, even the damn office staff had left him. Only Sidra remained, and now, she was on her way out the door, too.

He pulled into a parking spot in front of the store, and Sidra dashed to the car, shopping bags in hand. She kept her head down as if afraid someone would start shooting at any moment. That's how safe he'd kept her, he thought bitterly. So safe she'd been caught in a hail of gunfire twice in as many days.

"Are you okay?"

"I'm fine. Are you?" She was looking at him closely, worry lines forming between her brows. "You look kind of pale."

"I'm fine, too." He tried to sound casual. "Everybody's fine."

"Okay," she said with a shrug. "Whatever you say. Thank you for coming to get me."

"You don't have to thank me, Sidra. Did you really think I might leave you to fend for yourself?"

"No." She sounded genuinely confused by his simmering anger. "Why are you mad?"

"I'm not mad. I was just worried. You know, you were just kidnapped out of our yard a few days ago. I think I'm entitled to be a little concerned when I wake up and you're nowhere to be found."

"I'm sorry."

He looked around, spotting only one car that seemed out of place. "Is that them?"

She followed his eyes to the silver luxury car with dark, tinted windows. "Yes."

He backed out and drove away slowly. When they reached the next street, he waited to see if the other car followed. He didn't have to wait long, and as soon as he saw them, he turned onto the street that led to his parents' home.

"Where are you going?" she cried. "You can't show them where you live!"

He paid no attention to her but continued to drive toward his childhood home. It was time to end this now, and there was where he would have the most backup, the most people willing to keep Sidra safe.

He turned his head so he could look into her eyes.

"When we get home, I'm pulling as close to the steps as I can get. I want you to run inside. Do you understand? Don't stop, and don't waste time looking around. You just get in the house. Please," he added when she would have argued. "I just need to know you're safe."

"Fine." She grabbed his face and kissed him on the mouth. "Do what you've got to do."

He raced his car toward the house, barely stopping for her to leap out. Before she could get through the front door, Teddy was there with gun drawn, pushed her inside, and took her place outside.

Shaking like a leaf, she staggered to the stairs, where she sat on the bottom step waiting for the shooting to begin.

"What in the world is going on?" Betty shouted from upstairs before footsteps sounded on the stairs.

While Betty dropped down beside Sidra, Frank rushed to the porch with a rifle in his hand.

"Do you always have this much excitement following you around?" Betty asked her casually.

"No! And I hope it ends really soon. I don't think I can take much more of it."

The sound of car doors closing nearly stopped Sidra's heart. Where was Levi? And what would happen if whoever was following her came into the house? What if they killed Teddy and his father? Betty? Was Levi already dead?

Steps on the porch, followed by the low murmur of voices, and she was up, rushing forward, heart pounding, as her eyes searched for Levi. She grabbed the door post to keep steady as her knees went weak with relief.

Levi walked slowly beside an elderly woman leaning heavily on a cane. She wore an immaculate forest green skirt and sweater set, with a matching wide-brimmed hat over her white curls. Gloves, hose, sensible green shoes, and the string of pearls around her neck completed her outfit and gave her the look of the distinguished aging monarch she was.

A young dark-haired woman followed behind Queen Marie, her hand in the crook of a handsome blond man's arm. She knew at once who they were, recognizing Philippe's striking blue eyes as he lifted his gaze to meet hers.

Feeling overwhelmingly underdressed and ill-prepared, Sidra remained where she was as the small group mounted the porch steps.

"Your Highness, this is my father, Frank Tanner, and my brother, Teddy. Dad, this is Sidra's grandmother, Queen Marie of Medelia, her cousin, Lady Estella De Leone, and her fiancé, Philippe Beauchene."

"It's a pleasure to meet you all," Frank said. "And forgive us the welcome. We were only trying to protect Sidra from danger. We had no idea you were coming."

The queen smiled warmly at him, melting Sidra's heart as she said, "There is no need to apologize. We are eternally grateful to your family for keeping Sidra safe. Everyone wanted me to stay in Medelia and wait for her, but I found it impossible to do so. I insisted we come to America straightaway."

She lifted her eyes to the door, and her gaze locked with Sidra's. Whatever Sidra had expected, it wasn't the love that shone from her grandmother's eyes or the joy that lit her face.

For a moment it was as if no time had passed at all, as she gazed into the familiar blue depths. Then, suddenly, all the years they had lost were there again, and she was overcome with emotions she hadn't really expected to feel. How could feelings lie dormant for so long, only to spring to the surface at the first opportunity?

"Sidra! My love! After all these years! You look so much like them, Jeanne and Rupert. A more perfect mixture I have never seen."

Sidra pushed open the screen, and her grandmother stepped into her embrace. Tears streamed down their faces as Sidra savored the distantly familiar scent of her grandmother's perfume and the way it felt to be wrapped in her arms. Love poured from her in waves and filled the empty spots in Sidra's heart and soul as they spoke quietly in the language Sidra had never forgotten.

"You still remember our language," Queen Marie marveled.

"Yes. I forgot many things since being abducted, but I remembered the language quickly upon hearing it."

"It seems there are many, many things we need to discuss, but first, let us all sit down and get to know one another."

Looking impressively unperturbed to have royalty visiting, Betty showed them into the living room and rushed to the kitchen to brew coffee and tea.

"Your cousin, Estella De Leone, and your fiancé, Philippe," the queen said with a motion in the couple's direction.

"Philippe. I remember your eyes now—much more blue than green."

"Is it true Vincente Mateo posed as me?" he asked. "That he intended to force you to marry him?"

"Yes."

"Did you remember our betrothal?"

"No. I remembered only that you were my friend in childhood." She didn't miss the way his hand wrapped around Estella's or the worry that marred her pretty face. The feelings they had for each other were strong and thick around them, and she breathed a hefty sigh of relief.

Should she back out of the betrothal, she was certain Philippe would not argue. As a matter of fact, he would probably be grateful.

"Estella, I am so sorry about your parents. Especially since if not for me they would never have been in America at all."

"I have had little contact with my parents in recent years, Princess. For me, the loss of them happened long ago." She looked toward the queen, as if seeking permission to continue speaking. At the slight incline of the snow-white head, she continued. "I have been raised in the castle by the Queen since your abduction. It was imperative that someone be brought up to take over, should the need arise."

"Miriam and Gabriel were banned from the castle following the death of your mother," Queen Marie explained. "I had long suspected their hand in your abduction and, in turn, the death of your poor, brokenhearted father, but when my beautiful Jeanne's car was forced over the side of a mountain, I knew exactly who was responsible. Though I lacked the proof required to try them, I deemed them guilty in my own mind and forbade them ever to step foot onto the palace grounds again. Unfortunately, your mother trusted Miriam enough to show her the picture of you she received four years ago. From that moment on, they have wanted nothing more than your death."

"What did they hope to gain?" Sidra asked.

"The crown, I suppose. Miriam believed I could not change the order that the queen be the next linear female. However, I was well able to change it, and I did after Jeanne's death. Even had she killed us all, Miriam would never have been the queen of Medelia."

"Do you believe it was Miriam who tried to have me killed?"

"I have no doubt it was, although I suspect she was urged to do so by Gabriel," she said. "I have given the orders required to keep you safe, and Medelia is ready to welcome her Crown Princess."

Sidra's face paled at the Queen's implications.

"How can we be sure she's free from danger?" Levi asked, his dark eyes watching Sidra closely.

"There is no one else to gain anything from her death."

"You had Miriam and Gabriel killed?" Sidra croaked.

Her grandmother placed a gentle hand on Sidra's knee. "Gabriel was an evil man, darling. I'm quite certain he killed Miriam. Killing him was the only way to make certain you were safe."

Sidra glanced toward Estella who sat quietly studying her hands, no sign of distress on her pretty face.

"What about the man who tried to abduct me? The one who sent me the picture of my nanny?"

"He has returned to Medelia," the queen told her. "He was Mateo's lackey, and he returned the night that evil man died."

"If he worked for Mateo, then he wasn't trying to kill her, was he?"

"No. If there were attempts made on her life, they were orchestrated by Miriam and Gabriel. Mateo wanted to marry her to gain control of the kingdom. He may have killed her later, but Miriam and Gabriel needed her to die before anyone knew she lived."

"Miriam and Gabriel led us to believe she was sent to America by her father and was to be hidden away until she was old enough to marry. Is this true?"

Queen Marie gasped and shook her head. "No! Rupert had made some plans for her to travel with the nanny to America, to visit the nanny's sister after Christmas. They were to stay here only long enough for the Mateos' outrage to calm following Jerald's death. Rupert was heartbroken at the prospect, but there was no other way to keep her safe from them. She was kidnapped before Christmas."

"Why didn't Miriam and Gabriel kill me as soon as they realized I was still alive?"

"Miriam truly did come here at your mother's behest four years ago, to ascertain your safety until you were old enough to marry Philippe. I try to believe there was some good in Miriam, that perhaps she balked at Gabriel's murderous plan, but I can't be sure. From the day she married him, his wickedness began to stain her heart."

"Will you return home now that the danger has passed, Princess?" It was the first time Philippe had spoken, and she turned to face him. Both he and Estella waited for her answer with bated breath. Were they aware their desire and devotion to each other was so plain for everyone to see?

"If by 'home' you mean Medelia, I'm not sure." She looked at her grandmother. "I'm sorry, but I truly don't know."

"Of course you cannot make such a decision in a single afternoon, my child. We will be here for another day. There is a lovely bed and breakfast in town I would like to stay in. You can find me there, if necessary."

"What will happen if I don't return to Medelia?"

"We have been planning for that contingency for many years," her grandmother said with a soft, sad smile. "Estella is well able to take my place on the throne. If you should choose not to return, your bonds with Philippe will be broken, and he will be free to marry someone else."

None of them missed Estella's quick indrawn breath.

"And you, Grandmother? What will happen to you if I don't return to Medelia?"

"I will continue to grow old and will eventually die. But the remainder of my years will be happier knowing that you are alive and well."

"I will see you tomorrow, then," Sidra said, helping the old woman to her feet. "I will have my decision made then."

At the door, they embraced once more, and Queen Marie spoke softly against her ear.

"Listen to your heart, my Sidra, it will guide you home."

The memory came so swiftly she was taken off guard as she heard her father's voice once more.

"I love you, my Sidra," he said as they walked hand in hand toward the carousel. "You must always

remember that Mama and I love you." He stopped and crouched down beside her. Tears pooled in his eyes, and he kissed her on the forehead. "You and Nanny are going on a trip to a faraway country."

"How many days will we be gone, Papa? Will you and Mama and Andres come, too?"

"No, not now. We will be here when it is time for you to come home. It may be a long time." His voice broke. "But you will have so much fun you will not even notice."

"How will we know it's time?" Answering tears spilled over from her own eyes. "What if I get lost and can't find my way home? I don't want to go, Papa. Please don't make me."

"You must go. It is the only way your Papa knows to keep you safe." He took her hand and placed it on his heart, and then placed his hand on her small chest. "I will know here, in my heart, when it is time for you to come home. No matter how lost you might become, your heart will guide you home. Learn to listen to it, my Sidra. It will never steer you wrong."

Sidra walked her grandmother outside, watching from the porch as she and Philippe and Estella were driven away. The afternoon was crisp and clear, and the air was tinted by smoke from a nearby chimney. She surveyed the yard, smiling when she saw Merilee and Coda crossing the pasture side by side and the horses grazing there under the trees.

She could hear the low hum of the Tanners talking, no doubt discussing her and her family. She closed her eyes and listened. This is what she had dreamed of all her life. A quiet, loving family, the moments of shared memories and emotions. In her heart, she knew she would never find that in Medelia.

Behind her, the screen door opened and shut. Levi moved quietly across the porch, coming to stand behind her. He wrapped his arms around her, pulling her back against him, and planted a soft kiss on the top of her head.

"Penny for your thoughts," he murmured against her ear.

"I'm thinking of home," she said.

"Medelia?" his voice held a wealth of sadness and dread.

"No. Medelia hasn't been my home for a very long time. I don't know that I will ever think of it as home again."

"You haven't been there since you were very young. When you visit, you may change your mind."

"No, I won't. Whether I'm there an hour, a day, a week, a month, a year, it still won't be home." She turned in his arms. "I've been searching for a home for what seems like my entire life, Levi."

"And now you think you've found one?"

"I know I have."

"Where is it?" He sounded as if he were holding his breath, as she reached up and pulled his face down to hers.

"Don't you know, you silly man?" She touched her lips to his. "My home will always be with you."

He let out a shuddering breath of relief and caught her mouth with his. Their mouths met, his soft and searching, hers more demanding, pulling promise after promise from him as she ran her fingers up his back and over his shoulders, enjoying the feel of his muscles bunching beneath her hands.

She sighed as she rested her head against his chest, listening to his strong, steady heartbeat. No matter what the coming days held, she knew one thing for sure. Her home was here, in Levi Tanner's arms, and nothing could ever change that.

"Welcome home, Princess," he said, a smile turning up one corner of his mouth, as her lips caught the other.

"I think you should call me Your Highness," she teased.

"How about I just call you my wife?"

"That would be perfect, my love, absolutely perfect."

A word about the author...

Gloria Davidson Marlow is the author of several romantic suspense novels. She resides in Northeast Florida with her husband, works as a paralegal at a local law firm, and spends as much time as possible with her three grandsons.

Visit Gloria at www.gloriamarlow.weebly.com.

Previous Releases

SWEET SACRIFICES
WHEN SWALLOWS FALL
Both are available from The Wild Rose Press, Inc.
~
Flowers for Megan
Shades of Silence
The Butterfly Game
available elsewhere

Thank you for purchasing
this publication of The Wild Rose Press, Inc.

If you enjoyed the story, we would appreciate
your letting others know by leaving a review.

For other wonderful stories,
please visit our on-line bookstore at
www.thewildrosepress.com.

For questions or more information
contact us at
info@thewildrosepress.com.

The Wild Rose Press, Inc.
www.thewildrosepress.com

Stay current with The Wild Rose Press, Inc.

Like us on Facebook
https://www.facebook.com/TheWildRosePress

And Follow us on Twitter

https://twitter.com/WildRosePress

www.ingramcontent.com/pod-product-compliance
Lightning Source LLC
Chambersburg PA
CBHW070921180626
46817CB00003B/1158